Let's remove Andrew
and put Ron on the
$20 bill instead.

He's nicer.

Honest.

HEY
the fillet

ricky garni

HEY THE FILET was written between October 31, 2012 and October 31, 2013, and is a condensed version of HEY, which was published in conjunction with its slender brethren.

The poems are arranged in chronological order of composition.

Goudy Bookletter 1911 ten point font was the primary font employed in its composition.

Goudy Font was conceived by Frederic W. Goudy at the turn of the twentieth century. It was originally distinguished by the lozenge-shaped dot which appears over the 'i's.

The author would like to thank the following people for making it possible to complete this work, for their acts of kindness as well as for the memories we've shared: Dorian D'Agati, Amanda Thompson, Kitty Pilch-Hopkins, Kris Pass, Kitty Moses, Ken Soo, Jamie K. Sims, Amanda Lindsey, Dev Palmer, Dan Uyesato, Tara Lynne Groth, Linus, Margaret, Dashiell, and finally, Mitch Easter, for the kind gift of a wonderful typewriter.

Gomez: How long has it been since we've waltzed?

Morticia: Oh, Gomez... hours.

TABLE OF CONTENTS

To Faye

LOVE LETTER FAINTING OVER YEARS

In my thought, you are wearing a sweater the color of a fish
in a black beret crossing your legs on a yellow floor
adjusting the crown on your head and smiling in a sailor's outfit
while looking a little nonplussed and not smiling
while your glasses fall down your nose a red v shirt on your torso
while wearing a blue tank top in your skin so pale because are saying
ta-dah! with your glasses on ta-dah! smiling on stage at night oops suddenly
shopping at the bazaar as in the morning that you took off your shoes
and walked to the archway and into the water down you went
looked over your glasses when you think of that day in vertical stripes
and a stitched sweater the color that cream likes smiling at the puppy yawns
and the kisses into the field while you step forth and back over your shoulder
you look to see if I am still there: *I am.*

GIRLFRIEND

There must be a rule somewhere, that if you have
the most amazing girlfriend,
you don't have to write love poems,
all you have to do is show everyone her photo:

Look!

There she is, sitting on the floor wearing a cowboy hat, waving.
Isn't she the most amazing thing you have ever seen?

I am talking to scientists, professors, composers, acrobats, handymen,
chefs, bakers, sailors, gangsters, hobos, raconteurs among others.

It's hard to hear what they say: they all seem to be talking at once
I try to listen and then I just laugh, really–it doesn't matter–
I know what they are saying. What else could they say?

Isn't she amazing?

After a while, they even begin to look like her–well, to me they do.
After a while, Everything does.

Isn't she something?

I LOVE OLD LADY HANDS

I love old lady hands. I wouldn't know this if I didn't love shaking hands
so much. I love shaking little boys' hands, and girls', young men's and
women's and old men's and of course old ladies' hands. I didn't know
how much I loved this until I shook my first old lady hands. "My!"

I exclaimed, "My, but you have a wonderful hand!" She was old and
beautiful and had a wonderful hand. "What?" she asked me. "I said..."
Oh, why bother telling tales to a person or part you love, I always say.
The little boy walked away with her resting on his tiny, beautiful arm.
She was almost smiling and I pretended not to hear.

PROPHESY

Light was originally designed to be
less bright than it turned out to be.

STRATEGEM IN DEFENSE AGAINST STEEL

The small mustache awaits the guillotine.
Every day. One day will be his last.
Could it be this day.
Every day could be this day.

But all is not lost.
The small mustache is hoping to plead.
And the small mustache is hoping he falters.
That he delays. That he obfuscates.
That he ponders fashion.

The small mustache is hoping: *it* will outlive *him*.
And that it raise a glass to his lips after a fashion.
And in a warm place, they will be together forever.

THE WISE BRAY

When the Schubert begins
and the donkey collapses

the lambs start to gather
around it perhaps you think

the world will end
like a movie in French might

but you wouldn't know that
unless you waited to hear

who was weeping not why
in dark halls of popcorn

and purple velvet you left
earlier than the rest.

IF A WOMAN NEEDS IT, SHOULD SHE BE SPANKED?
News Clipping From The New York Daily News, Circa 1950

Miguel the counterman says: Sure, if they
can't behave and act like children,
they'll get the idea.

Frank the barber says: At certain times,
naturally. I have a lot of faith in the
hairbrush, when properly applied.

Teddy the parking lot attendant says:
You bet. A lot of women tend to forget
that it is a man's world. A good one
will help them get back some of the
respect that they have lost.

William the toy factory owner says:
most of them have it coming to them
anyway. An ounce of prevention is
worth a pound of cure.

Chuck the historian says: Good God!
Why would you ask such a question?
But now that you have I would say
Sure, why not? If history proves anything...

Michel the philosopher says:
I do not understand the question.
Please, don't ask me again.

AT TIMES

Sometimes we wonder if we are in jail
but we wake up to discover we are in an ox cart
and we go to sleep to discover we are in jail

The jail is never wet and damp
like an ox cart
and the bars go up and down not
all over the place like ox cart hay

Sometimes I am glad I am telling this story
to myself every day somewhere
in a wonderful spot
the size of a quarter
between day and night

Happy to keep things fresh for now
with animals that keep me awake
and happy to be where I am right now
and fine with where I am going

Waiter: may I please sit closer
to the window today?

DON QUIXOTE

I sent a drawing of Don Quixote to a friend. I had loved the drawing
for a long time and it was quite large, and you could see every beautiful
hatch mark that covered the knight's hand like silk. He also had one
perfect tear on his face, but that wasn't as beautiful. It had no hatch
mark, it had no design, no nature—just a simple, pure, pleasant oval
shape. I wrote a little caption on the drawing and it read: "I like his
hand, but not his tear."

I liked the sound of that, and even considered sending the caption
without the drawing. *What hand? What tear?* she would ask. But
I didn't do that. I sent the drawing without the caption instead,
and hoped she would decide to say something to it. She did:
but it was more about where Don Quixote found himself crying:
was it a stall? was it a jail? was the hay damp and warm? These
are the sorts of questions my friend would ask. But why pretend?
She's not my friend at all. I am in love with her. Am I just a hand
made of silk, drawing a tear that is less interesting than itself, myself,
uncertain of what to do with a pen for you? With a pen, you can
do nothing sometimes, but draw secretly for love.

COFFEE

People talk about being touched by people
at funerals but wouldn't it be nice if we
were all fingerprinted every day just like
at the police stations in the movies and
also probably in real life maybe before
we drink coffee in the morning if we
do drink coffee and orange juice if that
is what we drink and that way every day
or at least every night we would see who
we had touched with our presence before
going to bed early so we could wake up
early and have some coffee before going
to the police station or orange juice if
that's what we do every morning before
we touch people tomorrow and we will.

LOVE

Is as futile as telling two old ladies
not to laugh when they want to

TV GUIDE

I watch the old TV shows.
They do something different every night.
Monday night is Pinochle Night.
Tuesday, Bowling.
Wednesday, Bridge.
Thursday they aren't on. It's Fucking Night.
Friday, Checkers.

THE TRUTH ABOUT ETHYL

Just a few days left until Christmas and I still haven't bought my malted milk balls for stocking stuffers. I like to think of it as a tradition, but it isn't. It is just something I have done for years. The truth is: one year I forgot to buy malted milk balls and you know what everybody said? They said, "What's for dinner?" and "Did you hear that Ethyl was run over by a milk truck?" and "I have gonorrhea!" and "Will you look at this knife wound!" and "I love you but I am leaving you!" and "These slacks are a little snug in the crotch!"–not a word about malted milk balls. And the next year, I brought them back and everyone loved them and everyone ate them and Aunt Frances, Ethyl's sister, made the most wonderful cranberry sauce and the Japanese bombed Pearl Harbor in Hawaii where it was warm and sunny although it was lightly snowing in Brooklyn.

WE COULD BE LIARS

When José Feliciano was born his mother said: I want to name him
      "Unbridled Joy" but that wasn't possible because his name
            already meant that. Joy is a family name.

And so she said: What about Joe, Joe? My best friend bought José
      Feliciano for my birthday and kept him for himself.
            When I found this out I tried to be nice and I said,

"Which José Feliciano did you buy?" and he said "No no, when I say
      'I bought José Feliciano', I mean I bought JOSÉ FELICIANO"
            and apparently that's exactly what he did.

Now my friend tells me that wherever he goes, so goes José Feliciano.
      "C'mon, Joe," he says, "Sing us that song about being untrue
            and being a liar and lighting your fire" and when

He does, people start to realize that it isn't *a* José Feliciano
      but *the* José Feliciano, and a crowd begins to quietly gather
            around him and José Feliciano sighs,

Clears his throat, takes a deep breath, and sings that he would be
      lying if he said we couldn't get much higher in a voice that
            you can hardly hear because of the taxis

      And stupid dogs. Once he is through, everyone cheers
            anyway and smacks José Feliciano really hard on the
                back and kisses him on the face and he grits

His teeth and wonders if there are kissy smudge marks on his shades
and he clears his throat again which he so often does because
his throat is sore almost all the time because of the

Leash *estupido* which he feels like has been there forever and then
he looks up at the tall buildings and wonders where he will
be going next how much higher is higher but c'mon,

Baby–stop your lying, it's cold out there.
Do something. Do it.

IT'S IMPOSSIBLE (OR: WE'RE LOVERS)

I have never met a mission
that I could really call
impossible, but everyone
says THAT'S IMPOSSIBLE
and I say: yes, theoretically
it is, but theories aren't missions,
they're speculative reasoning—

they can be impossible all they
want to—in fact, they usually are
but when the imagination becomes
a mandatory endeavor, it becomes—

well, you see, that's where it can't be.
Let me state it more plainly:

My wife
is a fish.

I WONDER IF THIS HAPPENS EVERY DAY FOR 100 YEARS

A man rides a yellow bicycle through London in the morning.

THREE

One

I never liked David Hockney's paintings very much but I always admired that he wore very colorful clothes and his glasses were always big and round and his hair was always yellow. Some painters walk away from paintings but some people like David Hockney walk away and say I still believe in colors, I will always believe in them you see, I believe in them right now.

Two

Now that he is older, David Hockney has grey hair and wears grey suits but sometimes his shirts look like little swimming pools or pink flowers so I think that he is basically understanding something about grey and about colors you might say that he is evolving but I think he is staying the same. Normally you would say Oh that's no good one must change. But I think that's just what people say. I prefer to say something like Don't get me wrong you see I am happy. I am still David and I still love.

MARS & MY DAD

I want to turn on the TV and see Mars.
Father broke the TV with a hammer.
We looked through the cavity and saw the sky.
He pointed to Mars somewhere.
And Mars pointed back
holding a hammer
just so

ALL ABOUT STRIPES

If stripes meet stripes, they become checkers.
Unless black stripes meet black stripes, and
then they become a weave. This isn't peculiar
to black stripes: it also pertains to white, red,
green, blue and ... must I name all the colors?
I did that a long time ago and I felt old

after it was done. This reminds me of the
opening of Wang Chung's EVERYBODY
HAVE FUN TONIGHT: "I'd drive a
million miles / to be with you tonight" –
but I don't know why, recorded, as befit
the manner of the day, with drum machines.

No one uses those things anymore.
Is it a bad thing? No. The local movement
has taken hold like a virus and human hearts
flop on drumheads like deathbed flounder–

everybody has so much fun
tonight, but I can't see them
rightly. A million miles away they
seem, where black meets more of itself,

white says hello to white
even when you don't have to say it,
you just think it,
Wang Chung,
tonight.

ASK ME ABOUT THE HAMBURGER STAND NOW
Thank You, Emily

Brian Wilson sits around on the park bench for hours in Hawthorne,
California wearing a tee shirt that reads ASK ME ABOUT THE
HAMBURGER STAND NOW. Even though there are a number
of people walking up and down the sidewalk, no one stops to ask Brian
Wilson about the hamburger stand now. This is a different world than
the one Brian Wilson once knew. In the world Brian Wilson knew,
people loved to ask him about the hamburger stand now. In this world,
people drive very quickly and ask questions less often and more often
they are about God and the Ocean and the End of Things. In this world,
Brian Wilson is sad, not happy, and his tee shirt fits him very snuggly,
like the jerseys you see on bicycle riders who know that someday they
will win important races in countries that do not sound familiar, but
they might seem familiar if they did.

LOVE

Love
is not typed like this: ;pbr

Move your hands, it pleads,
and touch me again.

MIKE HAZARD

I prefer the pony tail to a pig tail when it comes to a doll
       that I buy for good luck or to stop the war or for my daughter
           as thought I had one, really. But let's be true:

the real thing I buy like one might Ginsu is Mike Hazard:
       he is a double agent, he is jointed and molded and blue,
           and he possesses exploding luggage

as should we all. You are probably wondering if he is an angel—
       why are you wondering that? Lemon chiffon is not what of
           he is made, but still I dream that someday I will touch
           his stiletto necktie,

hold in my arms his communication receiver-in-hat
       (I want to know the news like most men want to know
           the sports)—he is, oh wouldn't it be nice to be—
           a man of interchangeable weapons

I mean faces—you know, false disguises—enjoy if you will, he is
       prone to say—
           my bazooka launcher!
but look carefully: his words were spoken in 1965!

If you did in fact enjoy his launcher, you have long ago forgotten:
       the smoke is no more than a cockroach in the hope chest.
Open up your heart and see if the communication receiver
       is still working—

           I doubt it. Thank God for the trench coat
with secret pockets! with the assistance of nothing you recall,

you have walked on, turned around, smiled,

       survived, forgotten. No wonder you didn't cry
you smiled when,

    after all these years, your luggage exploded.

THE TOMATO'S LAMENT

Oh boy! A big tray of lettuce.
I know I keep saying this, but
can you blame me? Every time
I am about to stop saying a big
tray of lettuce, lo and behold,
there's another big tray of lettuce!
Man, I am going to sleep well
tonight–it's because of, well,
the lettuce. Goodnight. Goodnight.
Wait. Wait. Woe, Nelly!
There's another one.
It's really big all right.
It's a grand, lettucy night tonight.

DA DOO RON RON

Phil Spector is a famous record producer who shot a waitress
but before he did he locked the Ramones, a famous punk band,
into the studio for 8 hours and forced them to listen to his hit song
DA DOO RON RON by the Crystals over and over and over and
over. When they tried to leave he pulled out a gun and aimed it at each
of their hearts, one by one. One by one: that seems so romantic. But it
was frightening then.

And it seems funny now. That's Phil talking. He loves to say how
funny things seem now that no one thought were funny then.
Phil says: you know what things were then? Funny.

RESEARCH

According to the encyclopedia, the average day on Mars is 37 minutes longer than the average day on Earth. Also, the average individual has sex for ten minutes per sex event. And the average father spends ten minutes a day with his kids. And on average, a hot dog is consumed in three and one half minutes or less. If you lived on Mars, you could do everything you normally do. And you could have sex one more time a day, see your kids two more times a day, and have at least two more hot dogs a day. But you would die earlier because of all those hot dogs, but there also would be more people at your funeral because of all that yummy sex and don't forget the hot dogs be sure to bring the hot dogs.

FIGGY PUDDING

I had a dream that I was in heaven
and God was polishing me with a soft rag
My eyes were closed so the spray wouldn't
sting me and I was dead and shiny and happy
and smelled like lemon drops made delicious
by being so natural and fresh and truly divine
although pretend divine is divine, too

PARADISE

A prison of telephone booths float down from the heavens
pink, foam green, pale yellow

The sky is snowing little marshmallows that melt
on clean surfaces and only the dirty people remember them

Visitors drift down to get a better look at this parade
and are astonished to find nothing left

in the bumpy thick fields of lamb-white skulls
the music broken into half notes and rests

INGREDIENTS

Sage, my friend:
open the egg white door.

Kraken black rum and soften
the pepitas. Cocchi in silver,

drown me honeycomb then you my
clove, my rye, my summer, my end—

MY GOURMET MOUTH

I got my mojo working, but it just ain't working on you

These are the words of an ivory chocolate ganache
layered with wild Oregon huckleberry preserves
inside a milk chocolate shell tossed from side to side
that can't understand where things went wrong

AND TWO MISTRESSES

With nothing more than a dog
and two servants to protect him,
Petrarch chewed upon a green leaf
in the forests of Avignon

AND DOWN THE STREET

Boccaccio wanted nothing more
than a marriage filled with so much
laughter that he could perfectly paint
his wife's white teeth until they were off
white and so off white he could no longer
see them and so for us they never were.

DID THE BUTLER REALLY DO IT?

Someone threw this poem my way
by W.B. Yeats about a balloon
I never thought I would see the day
when stuffy ol' W.B. Yeats would
write a poem about a balloon
but he did and guess what? He puts
the balloon in a shed. Only a tidy
person, like a butler, would do
something like that but guess what?
'B' before 'Yeats' stands for 'Butler.'
So Yeats was just tidying up
as befits William Butler Yeats
The balloon that should be wild
and free and shot at by stupid kids
resides in the shed and the servants
have no key. Why? Because there is no
key to a shed. My Pappy always used to
say: to a shed, there is no key. Think about
that while you are trying to go to sleep tonight.
And then think about this: when Yeats grew old,
he neglected his butlery duties for the sake of art,
and looked like Charlie Chaplin and when
he wasn't laughing, he was wondering why,
holding a quill of dreams the color of buttermilk
and a sigh.

SCHWANENGESANG

I walked by the donut shop three times
and every time I did I said to myself
I really must stop in for a donut

Outside the shop stood John Wayne
he was smoking a cigarette
You must stop smoking! I cried

Was it all a dream?

Only if I were John Wayne–
One cannot never see one's true self

DEATH ROW

I am twenty six minutes late
for nothing.

WHITHER THE WILLIES

Once upon a time there was a terrible Willy. Or perhaps many.
Or perhaps they were very good Willies, indeed, decent Willies,
and when terrible things happened, they took wing and flew out
of the mouths of everyone who ever experienced such terrible things.
Forever will one miss one's Willies, but would one trade the experience
of terrible things and losing decency for anything else less terrible
that this world might offer? Sadly, no. Attention: this is your love song.

ICE CREAM

In old movies filmed in delicious places that you could eat like ice cream,
the plain girl is always beautiful, just beautiful, and soulful, and lost.
I once rated a movie 5 stars when a broken hearted girl smiled at a receipt
for her first lipstick, SEDUCTION, tore up the receipt, left it on the floor
and walked away forever from the man who she thought did, but never
did, love her.

FRAGMENT

...and I loved her dearly. How I loved to toss her against the barnacles of the sea. How I loved what the sea would then say.

TARZAN

On every Saturday afternoon at precisely 2:00, Tarzan
finds himself waist deep in quicksand. For this, I do not
blame the quicksand. Perhaps I do blame the quicksand,
but I blame it only once. A week passes by and once again,
there is Tarzan, waist deep in quicksand. Now it's Tarzan's
fault. Yet we are all creatures of habit; Tarzan is no different.

For example:

I once told a friend that in order to stop smoking, he must change
his routines, and he agreed, and he did. And now when he answers
the telephone, instead of lighting a cigarette, he watches Tarzan
sinking in quicksand, every Saturday at 2:00, for we are all creatures
of habit.

Last week however, the phone rang at two and there was only
quicksand on TV–no Tarzan. What could he do? He could answer
the telephone. It was Tarzan on the telephone. He had a terrible
secret to tell. The quicksand was crying. Tarzan had changed.
The quicksand was a broken man. The TV was dead. And he
had poured himself a delicious glass of sparkling burgundy brew,
and he had hung up the phone. The phone said, But it's not my time
to hang up.

PLACES I WOULD LIKE TO LIVE

On the red stripe of a blue and red stripe straw.

On a grain of rice in a chocolate bar.

In a smudge of turquoise ink in a letter that begins with *Dearest.*

Between the words 'worst' and 'was' in A TALE OF TWO CITIES.

In the chin dimple of a man with chin dimples (before he dies.)

On the sawtooth edge of the New York Times: January 1st, 1900.

On a slide rule that shines in the forest.

In the brain of a boy dreaming of a drawing of a palm tree.

In a blanket of onionskin from the Book of Job.

On a butterfly wing drawn by a butterfly.

On a hummingbird distracting Ian Fleming.

Next to a water fountain in the woods.

In a conversation between sugar and salt.

In the wind sitting next to a whip.

On a globe with the wrong names.

On the blue stripe of a red and blue stripe straw, too.

SON OF CONVERSATION WITH RED INK

Pretend you have crossed out every other word.
Pretend you spent half your life doing that.
Pretend the other you spent writing it.
What will you do if you cannot
divide perfectly in two?
Pretend?

MY CANDY BAR KNEW HOW TO DRIVE AND ALTHOUGH

His car was discovered in a parking lot near the Golden Gate Bridge,
his body was never found.

COWBOY TOMMY

In COWBOY TOMMY, Tommy's Grandpa builds a dog house for
Tommy's dog, Rover. It occurs to me that it is a good thing to build a dog
house. It is also a good thing to have a dog. They say that you live longer
if you own a dog. But if you must name a dog, don't name it Rover, unless
it likes to rove. If your dog likes to rove, it will rove. And if a dog roves,
don't build it a dog house, just name it Rover. For if you do build Rover
a dog house, Rover will walk out of the dog house, look at the name
"Rover" and it won't matter because dogs cannot read. However, if you
paint the word "Rover" over the threshold of the dog house, people will
read the word "Rover" and laugh at you and they will laugh at you a lot
and if people laugh at you, you don't live as long and you live even less
long if you own a dog and it roves away and you still have a dog house
that says "Rover" on it. But if your dog doesn't rove, and your dog likes
to stay, build it a dog house, where it can be warm and dry and comfort-
able at night. Your dog will be happy. You will love each other and have
good times together. He will lick your face and bark. And you can name
him Still,
or Cease, or Frozen, or Licky, or Happy or Barky. And he will live
a long life, and so will you.

BULLY MUSIC POWER

Looking at a painting of a lovely lady in a tulip dress playing the harp
seems odd when I am listening to someone miles away playing the harp
even odder when I see someone playing the harp on television, and I turn
down the volume so I can listen to the music once it moves from the harp
to the trumpet with its bully music power played by someone named Tulio,
far away and back, of course, once I turn it down and an angel appears on
television holding a trumpet-colored harp—or you know, harmonica—*of gold!*

KIKO VENENO'S WHITE MERCEDES

Translated Wrong

Three little rays sat in a boat.
The three little rays had a secret.
It wasn't a chintzy secret.
Here's the secret.

Moon rays,
that's not for us
that's us

HI, LILY!

Leslie Caron once wore
a silly hat and sang with
puppets that came alive
and then became puppets
again and then one day
much later danced with
both Baryshnikov and
Nureyev at the same time!
It's the American Dream
even though Baryshnikov
and Nureyev are Russian
and Leslie Caron wasn't
exactly American but perhaps
French. You never know where
life might take you, Leslie Caron
said to a British man wearing
a red carnation on the telly.
If you have great things happen
to you, you should tell the world.
It isn't bragging. I mean, is a
carnation bragging? she asked,
pointing at the carnation next
to his heart with a letter opener.
The British man said Yes and No,
Leslie Caron said No, it's not bragging,
it is just sitting there, not staying or leaving,
just being that thing it is.

A QUICK NOTE TO A FRIEND

Don't worry about not loving me. That's what friends are for. But I do
want you to do me a favor: if I am dying, I want you to kiss me on
the lips for a long time. Unless I am really smelly or am gurgling or one
of those things. If I am out of my mind, kiss me anyway. How do you
know if I am out of my mind? I remember somebody once said to me
"You must be out of your mind!" and meant it but I wasn't so you
never know for sure. So kiss me, once, just once, that will be fine.
Not now. Wait until then. I will kiss you back, too. I hope.
I will be very sorry forever if I don't.

THE BEGINNING OF THE END

And so I threw away my plutos
once and for all

FOUR MANNEQUINS I SAW TODAY

A lady cries in her black leather cat mask.
Her skin is like a pearl. She is fancy.

A lady with sunset pink coral eye shadow, I guess
that is a term, looks over her big nose and her red lips
like worms. She hungers for something, but who cares?

Covered in green are the violet eyes that indicate surprise
of lady #3. When I see her face, her complexion is like
barnacles on the bay wall, and I want to throw coconuts
into the sea in the morning.

A lady looks sideways in her denim-floppy beach hat
although not all denim are floppy. Hello Lady #4.
Her lips are perfectly pink and not wormy at all.
She has no ears. We laugh and often. If she were alive,
she would be humiliated. But she wouldn't be bothered
by our laughter nor our tears, which we often paint blue
for their infinities.

BRUCE

I used to have no particular feelings about action star Bruce Willis
but last night he let me ride around town in his ice cream truck.
"You want a cone?" he asked me, and gave me one for free.
It was one of those ice cream truck ice cream confections wrapped
in paper—a squishy cone and melty ice cream. I loved it and
was very flattered that he gave it to me. But before I could tell him
how much it meant to me he said: "We have too many of them
anyway" without taking his eyes off the road. He drove really fast.
He's a good driver. I used to have no feelings about Bruce Willis
but now I hate him and I think he's a good driver and his hands
are sticky and not nice and when I take his ice cream cone mine
are sticky and not nice, too.

OKLAHOMA 1957

A beautiful young lady in a scarlet dress
shyly looks down as she hands back a small book
to a crew cut alien boy wearing a bubble space helmet
and whispering I love you

The book is filled with handwritten messages
and they all say the same thing in different ways:

I can't hear that you love me
I can't hear that you love me

I love you too, she said

now take off
your bubble
head

OH BOY

L.L. Bean shipped my pajamas
to me. I hope they are white
with blue stripes. White, like
the clouds in the sky, blue
like the sky. Of course they
are. And they will ship them
in an airplane, that will be
in the sky and blue and white
and then land or crash on
the ground, the color of brown,
like the khakis I like to wear
that I order from L.L. Bean—
khaki-safe and rugged
fabric inside a flying airplane
filled with celestial colors
and moon beams
and many stamps
and dreams of
to America arriving.

THIS TIME IN COLOR

For their last movie, Stan Laurel and Oliver Hardy had a picnic.
There is a beautiful lake nearby with trees
undulating in the strong wind over and about their picnic table.

Stan and Oliver joke around
and Oliver pokes Stan playfully in the eye.
Stan is wearing a blue suit
and smoking a cigarette and drinking a cup of tea
and Oliver is wearing a simple brown tee shirt and trousers.

A moment later

Stan is with his family at the picnic and Oliver is no longer there.
Every few moments Stan dumps the ashes from the ash tray
onto the ground. Stan speaks with his wife Ida
and Oliver Hardy is nowhere to be seen.

Lois, Stan's daughter, is also there
and she plays with their cocker spaniel
pointing at the doghouse and laughing
as the little pup waddles in and out and
in and out. It is a very pleasant looking day
but Stan doesn't seem very happy–not a bit.

We will never know what he was thinking
because this was their last movie
and their last movie was a home movie
and it was in color
and it was beautiful
but it was silent

like the old days, only this time, in color.
Every once in a while Stan would look up from his tea
and say something. He seems to be asking a question.
Perhaps he is asking *Where is Oliver?*

Oliver is terribly thin. It doesn't seem right.
Stan is worried. *What's going on?*
Is everyone enjoying the picnic? Is everybody happy?

I thought everyone was at first.
We'll never know where Oliver is
or what Stan said. What did Stan say?

It is 1956, in Reseda, California.
The dog is barking.
Ida is showing Lois carnations.
The breeze is rippling the lake.

There is a tiny grape arbor.
The sun is a monster.
The more we look at the sun
The less it seems like itself.

TEN YEAR PLAN

If I had a child,
I could always
hide him in
the forest.

YOU'RE A GOOD DAD

But if we bake too many cookies
and we play too much soccer
we will be too tired to talk about
what happens to you if you don't
go to Heaven.

RING RING

The first man who ever lifted weights for fun picked them up
and then put them down and said *My God That Was Difficult*
and a thousand years passed.

A thousand years passed and then another thousand years and
why kid ourselves? A million years passed and someone said
Hey Wait A Minute and then one more minute passed

And the telephone was born, it was October. Ring Ring. Man says:
Who is this? Hears nothing. What good are words if there is
no one to give them to? Is this a game? The feeling of tremendous
weight came back.

A SPRIG OF LAVENDER, I MEAN HEATHER

Apollinaire would stroll through the streets of Paris and find beautiful things
and write about them with kindness and joy and great feeling in about 1915
I would like to think he would do the same at any time if he were here
today and saw the beautiful rain and mist which I ignored he might see
glory in it and scribble it down with his plume. And if he didn't throw it away
and he published it someday I could find it myself—were I to survive—and love
him all the more. But what if Apollinaire were a caveman? Yes, what if
he were a caveman? Would he do it then? Would he still have a moustache
and a bowler hat?

CLAMATO, THE ELIXIR

Helen walks along the road and finds beer clamatos,
which is just a fancy way of saying beer, clam, tomato
juice. And a discarded goat de-wormer package. And
a dog, and his dinner, a rabbit. The road is covered
with washed grey stones and I would like to tell you
something about my day, I say, and Helen says, but how?
why? when? says Helen, of Troy.

~!@#$%^&*()_+ OPERA

scene 1:
a squiggle eyebrow-like mustache or ocean wave tingling

scene 2 :
baseball bat painted black balancing on its little nib very carefully

scene 3:
a smart back flip and right side up again is A

scene 4 :
tic-tac-toe falling over starboard it's the wind

scene 5:
a snake lies down on the railroad tracks and is squished under them

scene 6:
two fat boys talk at the fence they could almost be twins or vanilla drops

scene 7:
a mountain top lops off its mountain of snow it's alpine

scene 8:
intermission

scene 9 :
a star is run over in the sky by probably another star blackened in the sky
snow

scene 10:

take a fish lop off his tail and eyes and what do you have well you have a
fish I mean you have his soul at least for what it's worth oh well

scene 11:

a bench that is less than or minus from or is it minus to

scene 12:

two people meet and kiss sideways X marks the spot @ 45° and christ is
born hooray for that all right

JOHNNY DESTINY

When I was a little boy, I never imagined that someday I would write
a textbook. How could any human being possibly do that? They were
so hard to read, they were so complicated and smart, how could anyone
write them? And yet someone must write textbooks, I knew that, but
I never imagined that someday that someone would be me. And now
I am old and content with the world, my life, I love my wife and it
wasn't me.

A RISKY BUSINESS

It is astounding that we don't touch our noses
when we look at each other so closely
but what is more astounding is that when we don't
we still feel a slight pain in our noses
when we go our separate ways the nose experiences
phantom pain, like old soldiers feel in lost legs or loss
when they think of chocolate sodas at the drugstores
why he couldn't have been more than twelve—

Someday, I will be a soldier, a soldier says
to a little girl, slurping
or maybe, he says
we will, when
she sighs, he says,
or maybe, just maybe
we won't

THE FIRST WAVE

I laughed when Helen Reddy said
You can bend but never break me

      I was kissing a girl at the time she said this—
      lips that tasted like white wine. Let me tell

you: you don't want to kiss a girl who tastes
like red wine. That would not be a girl taste—
that would be a Charles taste—Charles:

      Manson. Or Bukowski. Or De Gaulle,
      Charles. You see, no good comes out of

any sentence that begins with the word
'Charles', and ends with the words 'red wine kissing' while

      somewhere in the middle there's Helen Reddy—
      strong, invincible, woman. She is my kissing partner
      in spirit you see. Charles Darwin approves!

I confuse kissing with listening
sometimes: some say I am color blind.
Yes, I am wise. And that 'with pain' wise.
I tend to agree with me. And
I agree with them. And they are fools.

WHO ARE YOU GOING TO TAKE TO THE PROM?

a conversation between two shirts

Regular Fit White Herringbone?

No.

Slim Fit Blue Bengal Stripe Non-Iron?

YES!

(Shirts understand 'shirt' words.
And the words 'no' and 'yes.')

HAUTE COUTURE

Button is something we often do to the sky—first

      Doubling then halving its width and breadth—making it one

Pinpoint drawn to the pupil in plain fact. If one could

      Twill words as we do want—a modern miracle—dreams would

Dogtooth dreams like fighter planes until only one rested upon the

      Herringbone Earth, reduced and purified by no less than a

                          breath of

Premium sublimation, the other—not so much. It's what we want:

    to convert the

Button-down to the

      Cutaway, to pleat possibility until it submits, to exact and

express the luxury

Oxford Cotton within us. Our hearts. Where are they, though, hearts?

      Classic and winged, they are—striped, checked or plain

beneath our shirts.

And a photo falls to the floor. A blonde girl in a red dress with Haring
stripes.
She's seems far away, with a plant on a tree stump next to her, an empty
glass
a silver electrical outlet with nothing there. Betty Boop is rowing in a
canoe
over the door. What you can't smell is the mozzarella in the skillet. What
you
can't hear are the cows outside at night almost sleeping. Cows loved to
sleep
How melancholy she seems to know this–and then, how far
away.
in 1983. And she's dressed for something special. It's hard to tell she's
pregnant!

STARDUST

Are we stardust? Are we golden? Joni Mitchell asked us
and we are in the song she wrote called WOODSTOCK.
And then Joni Mitchell said something else right away
but I believe I forgot what it is because when you are
wondering if you are stardust, if you are golden, it's hard
to accept more information in your noggin. It's only when
you decide that no, you aren't stardust,

you aren't golden, that you can begin to contemplate
other things and you do. But if you decide, contemplating,
yes I am, I am stardust, and golden, then you evaporate in the air,
and lovers see you in the night sky albeit fleetingly and it makes them
feel like stardust, too and for a moment they are filled with desire
(well, more desire than lovers' desire) but then of course,
they, too,

       wonder: *Am I stardust? Are we stardust? Well then,*

I love you and there is always the likelihood that they may be,
and that they won't be in love, loved, or anything else
for that matter, for much longer, and that their journey will be
a pleasant one, or that they aren't at all, because they aren't,
and they will start to think about other things, and go on with
their lives, and go to the grocery store, and buy a bottle of milk
and watch a baseball game, and say BAD DOG when Puppers
is bad and walking in the flower bed–all things much less fetching,
you might think, and you

might be right, but also, you might be wrong. This too, could be
stardust, and golden. And you? And you?

                    Or not.

JOB INTERVIEW

A perfect room has drapes and a double lamp.
As does the perfect brain. A perfect room, brain
has a map in it, and someone saying, "Where
is this place?" and then points to this place,
as one does with fingers to the troubled heart.

I bless you as the Romans might for your might
and fine dress and black shoes but I cannot say
I know why your rug contains such vibrant shrimp.

THE BEST SEVEN WORDS
IN CHAPTER SIX
OF WUTHERING HEIGHTS

"Hindley"

"Fresh-Complexioned"

"Thrushcross"

"Incurable"

"Flogging"

"Burial"

"Dairy Maid"

No. The Dairy Maid did not die from flogging.
She is still alive, and enchanting. It is Heathcliff
who is incurable, and Mrs. Hindley who is
fresh-complexioned, and the world which is
thrushcrossed.

ON THE DAY THAT ERROL FLYNN DIED ...

Oh how often we begin with those words.
Let us begin again.

It is 94 degrees in Los Angeles in October.
Fire imperils La Crescenta Homes.

The beautiful starlet Gene Tierney
works as a store clerk. In England

Queen Mary urges her son: *Do not
give up the throne!* In Canada, there is

a fresh breeze. The man who claimed
to be descended from mutineers sighs,

says: I was sure that I was, so certain—
and smiles an apology, removes his hat
and lies down upon the wicked earth.

BENCH PRESS

I saw a 94 year old man flex his muscles today.
It was tremendous. He looked like he wasn't even 80.
At 80, he looked 40; at 40, he looked 38. He grew a beard
at 20, but at 17, My God, he looked immortal. It's funny,
one would think one might be immortal at 94. But at 94,
you look 80, or less. At seventeen you say: I bet I could tear
a telephone book in half. Your friends, now dead, say "Do it!"

JASON & THE ARGONAUTS

Congratulations on the purchase
of your Brooks Brothers (Brown) Necktie!

You might want to know that this tie was built
by both Brooks Brothers, the elder, who we will call

Jeremiah, and the younger,
who will we call Franklin.

Wait. No. We will call him Harry.
No. Elijah. No. Harry.

Franklin constructed, or "composed" the necktie itself,
while Harry conceived of the precise shade of brown
that he thought best would suit your necktie needs.

Harry, also known as "Elijah" finally chose "Brown-Brown"–
an extraordinarily rich, creamy shade of brown. So brown
in fact, that it is almost black, yet in its heart, it is brown.

When Franklin saw the Brown-Brown he said:
"Don't you think that is a little too brown, Harry?"

And Harry said, "On the weekends, I enjoy the racetrack
and a cool parfait with my mistress, Angelica."

Franklin touched his toes and Harry said: "Brown. Brown."

Did you know that there was a third Brooks Brother?

It's quite a mystery.

His name might have been Jarabold. It's hard to say.

Your tie should arrive in the latter part of February.

It will have eleven polka dots on it,
as a tribute to Vincent Van Gogh.

Other celebrities who wore our ties include
Fred Astaire and some of his friends.

When Abraham Lincoln was assassinated,
he was wearing one of our finest suits.

On the day before Abraham Lincoln was assassinated,
he was also wearing one of our finest suits.

On the day after Abraham Lincoln was assassinated,
he was also wearing one of our finest suits.

He didn't think much of our ties.

The ram on his collar was magic, but not enough magic,
but that's a different story.

AT THE BALL

A dolphin can jump in waltz time.
Anything can be in waltz time. It's easy.
All you have to do is miss the last heartbeat

out of four. The last heartbeat comes,
here it comes, and you say, "I'm sorry –
what did you say?" And your heart

plunges back into the water.
It counts to one.

TRUE LOVE

I saw your twelve paintings yesterday
on the subway. Also, at the grocery store.
I saw them in the sky being attacked by
a bald eagle–I thought those were extinct!
I bought a book on ecology to find out.
When I opened my wallet, as to purchase,
I saw your twelve paintings in my wallet today.
And then they all flew away. I see them when
they're away. And when they're there.
It's funny, but sometimes I think I never really
don't see your twelve paintings everywhere I look
and then I realize I do, I do. I know I always will.
Until you paint them. Extinct is a made-up word that
comes from nowhere and is going back there as soon as it can.

GHOST STORY

As the sun begins to rise
I look up the spelling of *tousle*.
Here's why.

I walk outside in my bare feet
before the neighbors buy their *pistolas*
examine their needs
and I do things to my hair
and I gingerly pet the apple trees

MELODY MAKERS

To think that I might leave the earth
before I see my first shadow of a cricket.
Before I shake the hand of Buddy Holly.
Before ice cream, just once, with you,
that thing in life for which I scream,
for which we all scream.

THE SQUARE SNAKE

Equally dangerous
Slightly funny

More can
fit in a box.

MERRY RAREY FRUIT

The Turquoise Ixia
a rare color with an ordinary
purple belly button.

The Soursop Fruit
pure white with three owl eyes
its beauty takes away tumors.

The Angel Oak Tree
alive in the south, it pretends
to be an aluminum octopus in autumn.

The Blue Vanda Orchid
congregates in the tree church
like greek china made of snails.

The Orange Ackee
and its big eyes
part rabbit
part droopy hound
precious fleshy
and dangerous–
it's yummy.

BLUEBIRDS

The scissors on my tax voucher look just like ravens.
Or blackbirds. I am not sure which. Flying sideways.
Sideways definitely. I am certain. I have a problem. I spend
too much time looking at paper, and not enough time looking
at the sky. I remember reading this in a book filled with bluebirds,
the imaginary kind, bluebirds written in grey ink that once was as
black as nighttime and someday will be white as blackbirds in paper
snow. It brought me to where I was there where I wanted to be.
And then I turned inside, to paper, to hands, to grey acting as blue.

BLUE BONNET

When I talk to you on the phone, your voice makes me think
of a blue bonnet. A blue bonnet and a fresh crate of strawberries.
A sun, really yellow, like the one in the picture book. When you say,
"Hey!" and then "It's me, Faye" I wonder if it's you, Faye. When
I wonder if it's you, and I say "Is it really you?" you say that something
that reminds me of peanut butter sandwiches and whipped cream, the
most wonderful things, and I wonder if that's true, the most wonderful
things anyone can do, you do. And I wonder, because I love it, and you,
and it sounds like you are saying the most wonderful thing anyone can
say to me, from you.

MOLLY'S

There's a little place across the street named Molly's.
It's a restaurant but when you open the door there's a staircase.
Everyone can hear you walk up the stairs. And if you turn around,
everyone thinks, "My, but you are afraid to eat at Molly's." You
have to go upstairs to see what kind of food they serve at Molly's.
You have to go upstairs to see if Molly is just a made-up name.
There are no windows on the staircase and so if you want to see
the sky you have to walk upstairs and see if there are windows
upstairs. If you go upstairs, you will see Molly and food. You
will see the sky. That is, if there are windows upstairs. If you are
the only person upstairs, then you will have to cook for yourself.
I am waving at you from outside and you are now upstairs. Now you
know about the sky and Molly's cooking. It's homemade. You are Molly.
"Hi Molly!" I say. But the window is painted shut and green. Molly
always shuts the window green. It is your way, the way of all Mollys.

SCHULTZ

to Faye

All I remember of Bruno, is how he saw everything as lovely and gold.
Even when the soldiers began to followed him, he walked slowly and
carefully and wistfully admired the golden soldiers behind him.

LOOK BOTH WAYS

If the little boy is not run over by the marching band,
he will remember it forever. He will become a great
composer. If he *is* run over by the marching band,
he will become a great composer. A different
great composer. A composer who wears
a clean blue shirt.

DR. J.'S DICTIONARY

Pg. 160: the couple-beggar:
He who marries beggars.

You were two beggars
and now you are one.

Two voices and now
you are one. Two

pennies and now
you are one.

LENNON/McCARTNEY

I walked to the pharmacy
      and I felt fine. I often feel
        that feeling fine is a strange sensation.

I felt it then, and it concerned me,
      but I still went into the pharmacy.
      And I talked to the pharmacist
      about all sorts of things,

      including myself

which felt fine,
      better than ever,
but I did not talk about feeling fine.

Feeling fine scares me: I do not wish to discuss it.
                    I do not want
                    to mention it.

When someone says: "So, how's tricks?"

I like to walk towards far away   I want to meet someone who feels

      the same way. And who says,

"I feel fine." Just a minute,
      I want to see what their face looks like

      before they skedaddle,

to know what it means to say

I feel fine

                And then I want to

                                go away

      until I feel fine again, and I do feel

lawfully married, perfectly fine

      and it concerns me.

PRUDENT ADVICE

If you're going to have an affair
for God Sakes, don't keep your
bowling scores for God Sakes
don't wear big black boots
and yellow socks after dark
in a neighborhood filled with dogs
not to mention

Beware! Over Yonder!
Curious and lively are the honey bees!

TESLA IS A BRILLIANT SCIENTIST

His nose is large and hangs over his face.
His cheekbones are shaped like a tallywacker.
His ears are quite huge and life-like.
His wrinkles look like a football.
His lips are pursed when closed.
His eye sockets are deep like a cave.
He doesn't say Ask Not What Your Country
Can Do For You.
He is astounding.
He is a brilliant scientist.
He says, "Watch this!"

WOW!

He has a death mask.
With football wrinkles.

IN THE YEAR OF THE VIDEO RAM

I turn left and crawl under a bridge, right and I jump over a lake, straight and I slide down a rope, right again and I jump over a fire, straight and to the side of a swirling jigsaw.

I have done this a thousand times, and then I stop and turn it off. When I am asleep, I turn right and cannot find the bridge, nor the lake, nor the rope, nor the fire, nor the jigsaw. I have done it a thousand times. It's only when I am awake, and alive, that I can laugh, in the lake, in that fantastic lake, where I stop, insist to everyone and no one that I am laughing, with burnt hands and a troubled spine.

I LOVE THE BIBLE

I love the Bible because its pages are so skinny
and they smell like shortbread and the Bible
it feels a little like an alligator and is the same
color as the mask of the Lone Ranger which
makes you think but then you don't if you fluff
it in the air it sounds like the wind and sometimes
a leaf will fall out and a word like *Thou* will float
like grace to the ground and burn, baby, oh so red.

A GREY DRESS

I love to think of the dust
on the lamp as sort of a
grey dress that I am too shy
to remove

DEAR AMAZON RIVER I WANT

A little notebook you can slip into your pocket,
that is always handy, that's nice and warm
when you put your fingers in your pocket
when it's snowing outside and you see
a big clock, and in your other pocket
a shiny pen you feel in your hand, and
the snow and that big clock and you say,
I hope I never forget this big clock
and this snow and this little notebook,
in my hand, in my pocket, and the other pocket,
the one with the pen, the one with the hole in it,
the street, the tinkling money falling everywhere.

I AM A SMITHY

I am a smithy.
If you have
to ask what

a smithy is,
then you do
not know
a smithy.

I do not
know what
a smithy is.

But I will
not ask.

Until I am
a smithy
no more.

NUPES

Oh the ceremony of
the bride and the groom
unwrapping a cheeseburger
once wrapped in foil

at the neighborhood
restaurant. It's an
excellent time
to forget

their first wife and husband
and all the loving patrons
that surround them

in the restaurant
that they will never
marry

and especially
those very few
that someday
they will.

POLITICS AS USUAL

I take pleasure in
the politician's
pink face

his blue eyes
the color of
a swimming pool

that contains chlorine

his slight eyebrows
that do not appear
muscular but instead,
slanted.

I am always astounded
at the number of colors
that formulate grey
in a man's hair before

they converge into a single hue:
snowy-white balm. I note this

in a man pumping gas
at the gas station
in his station
wagon—

not in the politician—no

he merely walks by the politician
who is wearing a jaunty hat;

rotund, his face is pink–
the cold air of the earth

in such a place one could say

unlike the other

he knows not of ice cream
          that brings the world to joy

SPINDLY INTELLECTUALS

What interesting names

for George Bernard Shaw
and Bertrand Russell

and their ill-fated meeting
on bicycles

George careened through the air
lands in Monmouthshire,
was saved

Bertrand was unscathed
save his knickerbockers
(his bicycle, also demolished)

George returned home
by bike
Bertrand, by train

and the two men
of England

lived for sixty years empirically
speaking although the truth is

in real terms
they were never quite the same

I AM A LITTLE

They call me Little Teapot
Not because I am short and stout
but because I am silver and very hot
to the touch and I smell like Earl Grey–
Earl Grey–this blond fellow who played drums
for the Funky Lokis and he was so crazy this
Earl he would say stuff like "Watch this!" and
well we would and we would cringe when he did
his cringe-making things we'd say: "No, Early–stop!"
but he wouldn't and he would do those things
all those things and his pants were purple like
those flowers in England that sometimes
make old ladies swoon back in the day
Boy Howdy! and swoon they did for
Earl in the Funky Lokis long ago
They swooned for Earl Grey
that's what they did
they swooned

A BREATH OF BREATH

This book is just a breath.
You breathe in before it starts.
You breathe out after it begins.
In the center is the book.
In the corner is a man
with a chef's toque
and a pen
and a breath
of ink
he breathes in
like writing
down
and gasps
and
trembles
for more
book

A COLOR CHART FOR AUTOMOBILES

The colors are quite simple, like Dark Blue, Pine Green, French Grey and Red. Each color looks like a little tombstone, and beneath each tombstone you see the year the color was born and the year it died.

Chrome Yellow Medium
1950-1964

New Bright Red
1959-1964

Fawn
1964

BICYCLE SAFETY, 1963

The miniature streets were filled with bicycles
     and stop signs and pretend buildings and parks
          and it was a wonderful way to learn how to be safe
               on a bicycle in a town that was drawn in
a comic book and which it was possible to draw yourself into if you

wished to but as you do remember that once you do you will stay
        there forever and your bicycle will be a creamy blue and just right
            for you and you will never fall down and you will ride
               very fast and your mother will miss you with
weeping until she draws her last breath which will be drawn small and you

have to ask yourself is it worth it and you have to answer Yes!
      it sure is and then you must tinkle your bicycle bell
           which is drawn to scale and you must ride
             and not wobble on the tiny right side
of the miniature street and smile a new world smile into a new world

TEN SMALL POEMS

i

The green company changed
to red and then turned dark
at sunset

ii

I could hold it in my hand for an hour
and trade it for an hour or two

iii

the tiger had alzheimer's
was the only reasonable explanation

iv

like a swiss army knife
flying with geese in winter

v

the word love
mumbles like
unborn twins

vi

the light comes to divert
maggie of the ten bras

vii

respect the painter
who paints herself
and unpaints you

viii
my pulse quickened
when *it's a truck* rhymed
with *what a duck*

ix
she beats women
with shoes until
they look like her

x
doctors only know
what sculptors forget

LITTLE PINK MAN

With three blue eyes
and a catcher's mitt for hair

You remind me of the old days
when I would oil my glove lovingly
for tomorrow's big game
with the sun in my blue eyes, three

Times I would drop it and
my face would turn pink
as lemonade and

I knew that I would long
for this feeling someday

Someday like yesterday,
or today

Whichever day I could catch
more effortlessly
with my hair

DAYDREAM

It must be a happy happy happy feeling
to be super old and walk down the street
with your husband your wife on a spring day

hand in hand and with nothing left to do
It must be like walking on popcorn
fresh, delicious popcorn

kernels fully popped
with no butter or salt
to hurt your feet
to make it more delicious
than it should be

on this happy happy happy day

EASTER

I saw the heads of statues rising from the ground
and until I dug them up they could not be released
and their bodies would remain beneath until I would
dig them up, but I could not dig them up, and I worried
that their bodies would not be there if I did dig them up
so I did not. I placed paper hats covered with cherries
on their heads, instead. Allergic to life, I waited
for them to sneeze.

A COCO-MEMOIR

I climbed three coconut trees on Brickell Point.
I wasn't very good at it.
It took a lifetime.
I was a little boy when I climbed the first.
And an old man on the last.
I was worried about my job and my kids
and growing old when I climbed the second.
I enjoyed that one the most; I did. I felt
like a coconut inside and it lasted for years.
And the ocean broke my fall when I fell.
Yet my milk stayed safe and deliciously warm.
and my wife saved me in her ocean dress
thanking me profuse until I died by
planting, of course, a fourth.

TWILIGHT SUITE

i

I wonder where everybody is.
Perhaps they are elastic and have
stretched so far that what I see
is still them but it's just a molecule
belonging to a heart or a lung.
When they scream I see the
tongue inside the heart and
lung. Crayons make this
smell young.

ii

I give one to myself, one to an angel,
and one to an angel painted red like
a devil. When he falls asleep, I wash
off the paint, and roll in it myself.
I appear to be candy, but I am not
alone that way. That's what they
say to make you feel better.
They are devils.

iii

Mr. Denton told us all about doom until
we felt doomed. Until we thought doom
was funny. It rhymed with room, which
made us happy, until we realized that
room rhymed with doom, and we were
in a room. And then we left. To a room
of outside. It was filled with gloom.
And stars. And more room.

ROGER

All I want to take with me on my trip to eternity
is the little souvenir of the Eiffel Tower
I brought home from Paris.

MY ABUSIVE BASKETBALL COACH
MADE ME A BETTER MAN

He taught me how to fix a jib
and tell a joke in French. And
let's us not forget that day in Spring -
all the 'i's before 'e's—*friend, believe, die*
Those he taught, too—while
seize, weird, vein—would wait for another day.

Yesterday he said would be tomorrow—
today brandished iron
in the form of a chair—
hear it come sailing

what I thought was once me
was just me once, and you
versus my open arms

AFTERSCHOOL

You must understand, I am from a certain generation. In my day
    I could tell the time. When I came home from school,
I made cookies and I made milk

    as might a cow. It's four. My parents never discussed sex.
It's OK: Four-thirty. Sex was hard to say, it's all the hard sounds
    that make it hard so you can imagine at the time of this life, covered

with Time and Life magazines everywhere which let's call
    the foyer. Milk and cookies to drown out the cookies drowning
in milk. Parents to drown out the sex but that was the time:

Now five. Children perhaps, but who is counting. That's life. Every night
    it was six according to the dinner table, my television on but of course
that was my head, mooing for answers from my Mom and Dad whose mouths

were silver flip tops if you squinted hard, the kinds that could slice your fingers
    and getting nowhere therefore but good but here's the good news: those
flip tops why they also were the world's most beautiful and cheap

(which means beautiful, beautiful) wedding rings–they promised something else
    but they wouldn't say what and did they deliver. Yes they did. Now it was
my time then. And then it was my time now. My bell begins to ring, just to think.

Seven.

LOUCHE

Comparative: more louche.
Superlative: most louche.

MAKE OUT

Of course, I thought immediately of a question: what do you make
this out to be? There is someone holding a map, or looking at a battle
plan, or inspecting a murder scene. When the teenagers make out,
forget the rest, they are holding a map. Think of the first time you fell
in love, and how easy it was to open a map, and how you relied on memory
to fold it back into place but you made a fool of yourself there and we
forgive you; by now, you forgive yourself. How could you have known?
Listen to the map: across the stream is a series of rocks; beyond the rocks
there is a road; the road is covered in tire tracks and debris. I believe it
is Route One.

UNTOUCHABLE

Eliott Ness was an Untouchable.
Until he married a girl named Well.
He became Touchable and she,
Well Ness. Eliott liked to touch
her unless Mrs. Ness wasn't Well.
This happened frequently, she wasn't
herself. One day, feeling a distance

Eliott Ness walked outside and fell
into a Well of Loneliness (no relation.)
And no one ever heard of Loneliness again.
Which is not to say Well isn't there. Well
Ness is there. That is to say, they found
each other. Sometimes

if you are well, you have dark secrets that are
so alone that you become them and no one can find you,
or even look, not even yourself. But you are still Well and
you are still there in Loneliness. Friends say, you are
Wellness even if by marriage, if Eliott finds you,
but if Eliott does, and could be right, he might say
"Well, I don't know where she is..."

LUNAR ECLIPSE

I remembered to do everything but cut my fingernails
and look at them on the floor and think of them like the moon
when I was eight years old and my head was out the window
at night we were going so fast that it was dangerous and I forgot
to tell the moon—I like that my fingers are just like you.

HE WAS WALTER MATTHAU SORT OF

said Faye

The Night That Walter Matthau Sort Of Repaired The Lock On My
Door In New York While A Weird Guy From The Christian Rock Band
Rock of God Waltzed Right In And Sat On My Sofa While Walter
Matthau Sort Of Worked On My Lock And How Walter Matthau
Sort Of Told Me He Wouldn't Leave Until The Weird Guy Left So
That I Would Feel Safe And How This Experience Led Me To Believe
That Walter Matthau Sort Of Was A Great Man And Also Handy
With Tools Although Now That I Think About It It's Possible That
He Wasn't Walter Matthau Really Sort Of But I Still Feel That Walter
Matthau Sort Of Was A Great Man Still Do Feel Safe Every Time I See
Pete 'N Tillie Is On Television I Mean Really On Television Or Even
Grumpy Old Men Starring Many Great Actors Sort Of Including The
Real Walter Matthau Not Sort Of And There He Is And Every Time
He Is Then I Think To Myself: "There Goes A Great Man" Sort Of

LADY GREY ON ICE

It's not like when you are young, and you still want all that drama.
You just want someone to hold your hand, and be warm there
and tell you everything will be all right, just like a donut would.
But not a Lady Grey On Ice donut.
An Old-Fashioned donut. Plain. Simple.
Look at how beautiful the sky is this morning
is another way of saying it
when it is too early to be awake
but you can still walk
past the neighbors quiet house
you can still watch the coffee warming the sill.

COFFEE THOUGHTS

If we put poison in the coffee
All the coffee drinkers would die

All that would be left were people
who didn't drink coffee

I imagine hundreds of people walking
through the fields

Picking up beans
in wonder and discovering

They're red, like cranberries,
not brown, like chocolate

And wondering if maybe
they should drink coffee, too

They should
Think of what they've missed

They missed for starters what
we did to people who drink coffee

And what we didn't do
to people who don't

QUEEN

Queen was a wonderful band
back in 1972. But I never knew
how easy it was to realize that
you are listening to Queen when
Queen is playing next door.
It doesn't matter if it is Boston,
Miami, or San Francisco:

Queen penetrates dry wall.
Queen manages to get to the other side.
Not just manages: Queen arises
from the sea foam resplendent,
with aplomb and finesse, adjacent—

into the ears of the neighbor goes Queen,
and out of the ears goes Queen, too;
and then ...

Whenever I travel, whether it be
Boston, Miami, or San Francisco,
I always see puddles of notes
on the floor of my apartment
and emptiness next door. I know
what has happened, and

It is majestic, and I am
the kind of neighbor
who does not look
at the floor and
weep.

OUTDOOR EGGS

for Faye

I am flying through white
and in the middle of the white
is a little patch of yellow
just a little patch, and then I dream
I am flying through more white, more white,
more white I do love white, but it is for only a moment
that I feel the little patch of yellow, but I do not know
if I would be happier if I flew without ever knowing
it at all, but there is barely time to think about that:
far in the distance I see the big something,
the tiniest patch of blue.

HOW TO TELL TIME
A Golden Book Review

I learned how to tell time
by reading *How To Tell Time.*

The cover was black and there
was a golden Gruen Precision Watch

in the center. The Gruen Watch
had hands you could turn

as long as you want until they fell off.
They didn't have to fall off but sometimes

they did. The best thing to do with
How To Tell Time was to walk around

the clock and see all the interesting things
you could see. You could see five little pictures
of one little boy and one little picture of one little girl
as they had various adventures around the clock.

If you walk clockwise, you see the little boy
wakes up and puts on a yellow shirt and looks
at his sundial and it is something o'clock and

his tabby kitten purrs under the shade
of the sundial. Then you see the little boy

puts on a white shirt and ties his shoe
while sitting on the world and a red

and white striped candle burns down slowly
and regularly. Then the little boy changes into

a red shirt and reads a book in front of his desk
without moving his lips until he puts on a green shirt

and this time a blue cap so that he can run and run
in the sun until he is so hot that he takes off all his clothes

and jumps in the water and smiles because he is naked
and timeless in the water is it a beach is it a lake is it a
pool is it a stream is it a pond is it a swamp? Well, there is

a little girl playing with a bucket in the sand wearing pink
and so it is a beach. There is a little star next to her.
The star is light years away from us now.

Don't be sad Me! Look! Then there is a little boy again
and he is in a yellow shirt again looking at his sundial

and his tabby cat is purring again and soon he will put on
a white shirt again and tie his shoe,

again. Did I mention he is wearing blue pants?

COCONUT-SPIKED PORK WITH QUINOA & PEANUTS

Let's think about this:

Coconut: A nice tree. It curves when it's near the ocean.
The fruit is husky shelled and golden brown. It was once
a Marx Brothers movie. Groucho added an "S" to it so
that everyone could be a coconut. Coconut. Oddly not
a term of endearment. Why? The fruit is white as snow
and every bit as sweet. Sometimes inside or enrobed by
chocolate. If you bring a coconut cake to the office,
no one will eat it. Everyone will say, "Yuck! I hate
coconut!" George Harrison once opined: "Coconut
Fudge really blows down those blues." Coconut: grows
in Thailand. When the weather is magnificent, coconuts
go everywhere. Little baby coconuts are like hand grenades.
Coconuts shine in the sun. Coconuts can cover breasts.

Spike: something with a football. Also, the great film
director Spike Lee. Spike Lee once saw the movie
ROCKY wherein Sly Stallone told Talia Shire that
there were a real pair of coconuts, although not really.
Spike Jonze: another film director. Never saw Rocky.
Spike Jonze never ever spiked a football. Spike Jonze
found Palm Pictures. Palm, like coconuts.

Pork: belly. A commodity. A word. Funny sounding.
Yummy with pear chutney.

Quinoa: who knows? Little, pale.

Peanuts: getcha red-hot.

NOBODY WANTS TO HEAR HOW MUCH YOU ARE IN LOVE

It's 2011 and I fell in love and discovered something horrible:
nobody wants to hear about how much you are in love.
Believe me, I tried. You can try too, but they will change
the subject or give you a funny look. They might be in love
as well,

but they aren't in love with you talking about being in love.
They might not be in love, and still the same holds true.
They don't want to hear about how much you are in love
and the ways in which you are in love.

But imagine if you met someone who fell in love with
what you said about being in love, and how that might feel,
and how they feared that their love might go away
if you stopped talking about how much you were in love

And the terrible responsibility that might hold. If you stopped
talking, they might die. When your heart is broken because your love
goes away, you just might die. No, you will die. You have to stop talking
eventually and then it is over. It is a good thing that nobody wants to fall

in love with what you say. At first it seemed bad.
It isn't bad. No. It isn't bad. Yes, it is a thing of excellence.

WELL YOU NEEDN'T

to Faye

Forgot my wallet
in the rain
on the way
to the store
for laundry soap
while thinking of–
of you

Although I probably forgot it
before I was in the rain
putting on my chinos
looking at your picture and
looking for my keys

Normally I would ride my bike
but it is raining–
delicious, mouth-watering rain
and laundry soap

is what I need
My car is nice and old
I like clean clothes
and I am thinking of, well, you

with no wallet in my hand
foggy hearted and near the frogs
perhaps I will go to the aquarium
perhaps I will see you

I am in the store now
It's daybreak
everyone is courteous
and wearing blue

Your hair is blonde
you laugh like a pirate
tonight perhaps you will
fry catfish
my clothes will be dirty
your picture must be you–

You. You. Good Ol' –

If I could change a thing
Here we go
If I could change a thing
If I If I

But
I wouldn't
No
I wouldn't

WITHOUT WIND, THERE CAN BE NO WAVES

Also, without wind, and waves, and sun, and
beach blankets, and bikinis, and Beach Boys, and
transistor radios, and Coppertone: there can be
no surfboards, although not necessarily in that order,
although that order works as well as any other. That
was my fortune cookie. I found it both wordy, and true.

THE WOODWINDS OF NEW YORK

Looking at the old photos of New York, the sidewalks were wider but the people were smaller. That's right: smaller people had more space in which to walk in New York. Now larger people must walk like children in New York. But children need space!

And ice cream. Luckily, New York has ice cream and small sidewalks that seem large when you think about them. What do you think about when you think about them?

Well, you think about....peppermint sticks!

MY SPANISH HEART

Look at Chick walk into the room through the door (wearing a hat)
It's the kind of hat that makes you happy to be in a room (with)
Now, land sakes, it is the rhumba (that is playing)

That would be Chick, playing the piano, so masterfully (well, yeah)
Or it could be someone else (not named Chick)
Who is it there tapping their feet (with ample breasts)?
Why, it's a(n) (ample-breasted) woman!
How I love them (the gods.)

Naturally. This is the scientific reaction to the sound of rhumba
(the tapping)
Of the feet, to the sound
(don't say waltz, no, it's something else what is it, it's)

Armando's Rhumba! Played by Chick.
Who among you know Armando? (Not me.)

Chick walks out at last. The piano is under his arm.
He is the only man (that could answer the question.)
But he prefers (to walk) with the piano (under his arm.)

Who among us does not (those who never do.)
Wearing a shirt of flames. (Better than it sounds.)
Hello (everyone!) Ah, (Armando.) Oh (God.)

SHEET MUSIC

I remember the day that I realized that lithe, black figure who lived
on the page in my notebook was just a quarter note. He was B-flat
and before I knew it he was gone as were his three friends.
They wore hats. They wore ties. Some were silent.

ECONOMY

Pat Sajak says:
let me answer
you in Spanish:

No

THE LESSONS OF ZORRO

If you wear a black mask, you shouldn't have blue eyes.
Brown eyes are best.

If you are drunk and filled with vengeance,
it take ten to fifteen minutes to learn how to use a sword
like a master if your secret hideaway is filled with candles.

Spanish things catch on fire all the time. It's the candles.

Candles make babies look sweeter.

Swords are great. Everyone should have one.

What is the point of a sword? Slicing through things
to make other things fall down.

Where is the best place for a head with a mustache?
A wine cask or better yet, decanter.

Use a sword to remove the head from the body.
Don't worry if the sacred heirloom necklace falls
blood splattered to the ground. Leave it in the desert
and someone will find it and know what it means and
set upon a course of vengeance for sure.

If you get close enough to a woman in a sword fight,
you can kiss her on the mouth.

And she can kiss you back on the mouth.
If you are close enough again.

It's fun to sword fight women with are named Elena.

What is more fun than riding one horse?
Riding 2 horses. 3 horses. No, 2 is sufficient.

Sideways branches from low-hanging trees
love stupid people on horseback.

The only Spanish word you need to know is "Zorro."
It's a Scrabble word.

So is Fox.

And Quotient.

And Quiddity.

Not "Debonaire" or "Lithe" or "Mustache."

The job description for evil Spanish Scoundrel Capitán Guard
is as follows:

Must look good in white, blue and red, and
must not know how to use a sword correctly.

Zorros never die, but they always seem to have saber wounds
on their torsos and seem like they are going to die but they don't,
although you can't help but wait for them to die. You get really
tired of them almost dying.

If you slice through the air three times you have a "Z."

Four times and you have an "M."
It can stand for "The Full Monty"

or "Moley." Or "Machismo."

It takes six times of slicing through the air
to turn a fully-dressed woman into a woman
clad only in her bodice and blushing a rose tint.

Be careful with fully-dressed women.

If you lose your daughter to a villain, wait twenty years.
He will die and she will call you Daddy and everything
will be fine but then you will die from a saber cut that
you seemed to be dying from forever.

In a handsome contest, Antonio Banderes beat
Anthony Hopkins. And in the next handsome contest,
Anthony Hopkins beat Antonio Banderes.
Their eyes are blue and brown, respectively.

You can sword fight as many evil men as you want,
but never kill more than three.

Always let the villain drown in his own golden ingots.

Or drive a sword all the way through their bodies
and make sure they fall backwards and listen to everyone
scream "YUCK!" even though, after all, they are dead
way before that.

Lead a cautious life.

Eat fleshy fruits.

Don't try to decide who a villain is by looking for a mustache.

Everybody has a mustache.

I have a mustache.

I am stroking it as we speak.

It looks distinguished.

Trust me.

SAVAGE WATER

My Eau Sauvage is on its way!
Today it is in Anaheim, tomorrow
it will be on a truck, covered in wrap,
cardboard, brown tape, postage stamps
and handwriting. Beneath all of that will be
Eau Sauvage in a rippling bottle, lightly tinted
green. It will smell like limes! And basil and cumin
and orris rosemary amber! Once I gave a girl named Mary

a rose, it's true. But today I want to give a girl named Faye
a sweeter, more savage-smelling me. *Eau Sauvage!* I say. But
I must wait for Anaheim: for its cardboard and brown tape,
its postage stamps and handwriting, its truck driver who eats
potatoes, curses for free, who walks to my door in brown shoes
and smells like rosemary and naturally, brown shoes. I must wait.
I must wait for days. I waited for years to fall in love. Why do
I hate waiting for days? You understand, don't you? Even if you
do, even if I must, then you still must listen to me and wait, and
for years, and for a few days more for this, and for that, I thank you.

LITTLE FAYES

i

I met Faye today.
It was in May.
Faye, I used to say,
What is today?
It is Faye Day,
Faye say, one
day, today,
but not
in May.

ii

Would Faye love me
if I wore a toupée?
I cannot say. Neither
can, or will, polite Faye.

iii

Once I told Faye
my heart was a
soufflé. A soufflé
of parfaits? Yes,
for you, a love soufflé,
dressed quite snug
and for reasons unknown,
sautéed.

iii

Faye used to play
the flute flambé;
ce qu'est une flûte!
that is a flute
with flames
of French:
zestily, me,
they disobey

iv

I sent Faye
a communiqué:
Please - if you can
or may:
return to me
my Chevrolet.

v

Faye dreams
of a world
faraway -
replete with
the most savory
of Sauvignons—
those of Cabernet

vi

Faye, I asked,
si vous plaite—
honor and obey?

vii

The floors of parquet
and their bouquet
are missed by no one
more than by Faye

viii

Knowing Faye is like reading Dante
but not the bad Dante, so cliché -
no - the Dante we love, of heavenly,
oft rosey, *soirées*

ix

Rather than Faye,
Faye wishes to be Philippe,
Philippe of Paraguay
or a brother of Nicholay,
or a lover of Hemingway
anyone, says Faye
any day, anyway
other than Faye

x

I would invite Faye
to my chalet
but my owning a chalet?
Mon Dieu! My chances
are less than the ghost of a

xi

If you saw the dancing Faye
you would never think or say:
Dios mio! Is that an *hombre?*

xii

I awaken early
and prepare to make hay
by spending my morning
writing of Faye–for
he rest of the world
I must demure and delay;
the world, I shall save,
for a much more rainy day

xiii

Faye plans a stealthy getaway
through the breezeway
does it work? No way!
There are no hoorays to convey
for Faye missed the breezeway
and is trapped forever
in the desperate place
a/k/a:
the silent sorbet

HOW I SPELL WIND

to Faye

I walked downstairs three times to see if you had written me.
In the old days, I would have walked outside and waited.
It would have been so dark. The morning light would have
woken me up, and that bluebird that flies near your tree
would pass and I would ask: "Did the wind vibrate as you
flew by her house? Did it feel like her name? Did the first
letter of the wind begin with an 'F'?"

LETTER TO A FRIEND ABOUT DELL COMPUTERS

and a response to the question: Do You Like Strawberries?

Remember: 'Dell' rhymes with 'Pall Mall'–
which means chaos, confusion, or smooth,
refreshing cigarettes in burgundy-colored boxes,
which rhymes with 'foxes', which are foxy,
which are, according to Jimi Hendrix, ladies.

I do like strawberries a little.

A NAP AT MIDDAY

A nap at midday and you wake up and wonder
What time is it? 12? 3? 7? 21? 43? Hike!

It's Thursday: your mother rises from the dead
and makes you pancakes. They are delicious.
They taste better than they did before she died.
Years before she died, Mr. Bisquick died and went
to Heaven and kept working making perfect pancakes.
On Monday, he introduced himself to mother–who wouldn't?
"How do you do?" he said, "My Name is Orville Q. Bisquick"
and she said, "Fine, thank you, it is most pleasant to meet you!"
and then she said "I could sure use some help with these pancakes"
and he said, "I would be happy to oblige" and he did, and what
transpired was amazing, and there you go.

MOTHER'S DAY

I see warm, beautiful temperatures
in store for me

mornings filled with chocolate
and coconut in ice cream

and strawberry and lime
in donuts

old department stores
and RX pharmacies
in the blinding sun

as a way to walk home
but not really walking

and poppy seeds

you can hardly see
but I see

too little to mean
anything

I see poppy seeds
more than anything

in the journey

in store for me

WRITING LETTERS TO AN OLD FRIEND

at an approximate address
his face is light blue
against a sky blue background
of everything blue,
she said, so pale,
so blue

OLD LOVE

You misunderstand me: I do not
love peaches. I ridicule peaches.
Perhaps you can't do that. But I do
scoff at them. May I do that? I may.
As for bicycles

and cheesecake: you are correct–
I would sacrifice anyone in the world
to have bicycles and a good cheesecake
(other than Faye, of course.)

And yes, I do like nougat. It's a fine
word, a good word, a naughty word
a word that–

It doesn't matter. Now I am thinking
of Faye. For her, I would do anything–
the rest may go.

RHODODENDRON

Someone called me from Brazil, he didn't mean to,
        and he just talked away. I tried to talk to him, too,
but I didn't understand anything he was saying, and I told him

that and then I told him other things and then someone from Brazil
        answered me and probably told me that he didn't understand
me either and kept talking and told me other things too. When he stopped

talking I didn't tell him that I didn't understand what he was saying
        but instead told him about this song I had heard that I couldn't
get out of my mind, and all about my neighbor who always says hello

to her husband before she gets into the house, and how to spell
        rhododendron after I told him how beautiful they were and that
they were in my yard. He didn't say anything for a minute after I stopped

talking, but then he started again, and told me all sorts of things, I am
        guessing they were about how life in Brazil was for him lately,
how hard it was to stay in love in Brazil, and how there are no

rhododendrons in Brazil. We both laughed at the same time and then
        we both said GOODBYE to each other at the same time and
then we both hung up. I missed him like you

miss an old friend, and realized he probably would never call again,
        and so I looked up Brazil in the dictionary and discovered
that Brazil was named after Brazilwood, that Brazil was once run

by a man named Pedro, that you can find Toucans and Jaguars
        in Brazil for they are plentiful, and

the waterfalls there are deep and lush, and will make you feel at home

right away, if you ever decide that enough is enough and go there
and leave everything else except your favorite beige suitcase,
behind.

YEAH YEAH YEAH

We were four years old and we went to the store and bought salted butter caramel ice cream and it was great and it melted really fast.

We were four years old and we went to the store and we ate coconut cake which was so yummy and then had another.

We were four years old and we listened to the Beatles and they sang YEAH YEAH YEAH and we screamed YEAH YEAH YEAH to the Beatles.

Now someone says The Beatles, Big Deal and they pass by the store and don't stop and there's a coconut on the ground and it's dying and we're melting.

SAM & THE FIREFLY

I discovered the magic of words when Gus the Firefly
wrote COME IN FREE SHOW and GO FAST GO SLOW
GO RIGHT GO LEFT with its conspicuous crepuscular use
of bioluminescence in a world that didn't exist—oh what a book!

the next thing you know
                  I was going slow

TIME MACHINE
Thank you, Laura

I awoke to your doorbell and your tray of chocolate fudge
bejeweled with colorful dinosaurs. I sat down and ate them
until they became extinct.

DEBBIE MILLER TIME

Cabbage, orange, lime, cilantro.
They form a nest.

And inside the nest is a bird.
The bird is a t-bone steak.

Everybody is coming for dinner.
There will be dill inside the potatoes.

The way the potatoes fit
inside the cast iron skillet

Reminds me of playing Sardines,
Sardines in a Can. Next to me,
I wanted to kiss Debbie Miller
of the checkered dress,
small white teeth,
brown eyes

But now it is too late. When my friends
come over for dinner, I will ask, as always

I do: does anybody know what happened
to Debbie? Does anybody know why
nobody does?

LET ME TELL YOU

Let me tell you a true story about the funniest man on earth
who sold pinkie rings backstage in vaudeville and whose father
was a jeweler and who sat in a tub with water up to his neck
and told funny stories to his dictaphone and who Groucho
called "probably the funniest man who ever lived" and who
Jack Benny called "the greatest gag man who ever lived" and
who signed a contract one day and was the funniest man who
ever lived and he was happy and sad and then he went to
bed that night and then he woke up the next morning and
died and had a deep subtle understanding of the foibles of
human nature and a nimble mind but he died and he had sad
eyes but of course that's what they say he signed a contract

FAMOUS MONSTERS

They say that my new Monster Magazine will be delivered by mail
tomorrow. I think I am going to buy a new car. I am going to drive
to the mailbox. In my new car. Everyone will say hooray! as I drive
to the mailbox. In my new car. If my Monster Magazine isn't there,
I will just die,

die, die away. Monster! Everyone will cheer. Magazine! There is
always something to be happy about, even if I die. Tomorrow
the Monster Magazine will be delivered. My Monster Magazine.
My new car. My beautiful new car. Monster!

.

EULOGY ON A BRIDGE

He was a beautiful person who enjoyed

ONE SMALL STEP

Something about landing on the moon made me a little sad.
Even the moon looked a little sadder after we landed on the moon.
The moon looked at our faces looking at the moon, and it became sad.
It's very similar to being in a room when someone yawns.
The next thing you know, you are yawning and looking out the window
and the moon is sad. That's because here comes the sun right out of
the ocean. You yawn and go to sleep. And the moon says
Good Morning, Good Morning. And the sun. The light.
Oh, such a happy day.

IF

If I could have all the movie posters in the world
that had rugged men in work shirts with Stetson hats
covering their eyes as they walk towards the camera
with five o'clock shadows or perhaps even seven or eight
purposeful and with a grim sense of determination to be sure
sometimes wearing a shiny star and sometimes not, well–

I would take those movie posters and wrap them in a cardboard
cylinder and apply the proper postage to the cylinder and I would
ship them to myself and I would wait and wait and have lunch and
while eating lunch I would wave and smile I would say, "What a life
this is!" and sit myself down have some dessert. Yum. Yum.
YUM! and wait and wait and wait for it.

YOUR HONOR

When they say 'the bullet left the chamber'
how can you not think of a shiny silver bullet
in black robes, slowly making his way to
a mahogany door with a brass door knob
and so feeble, so weak, so white hair'd of pate
that he can't open the door to walk out into
the sunny world easily enough to truly kill anybody?

BABY BOOK

I took my first break in 1962.
I sat under a shady tree and drank
lemonade. Then I heard his voice
saying Break Time's Over! and it was
time to get back to work and I stood up,
stretched, and started all over
and I made a hundred dreams
of trees, of shade, of lemonade.

AT THE DINNER TABLE

I like to think of the dust
on the lamp shade as sort of a
grey dress that I am too shy
to remove

PERHAPS THE BEWIGGÈD DINGHY...

What notions make you laugh
except for the obvious ones,
like Narwhal?

THE KLAATU DIARY

At breakfast the next morning, during
alarming radio reports, Klaatu takes in
his fellow boarders' suspicions and speculations
about the reported alien visit.

On a lovely day in 1951
in Times Square, New York,
The Earth Stood Still.

Everyone kept walking around
and someone went to Whelan's
Drugstore for a penny chocolate

soda and upstairs the Parisian Girls
were dancing, Parisian girls, dancing,
dancing. Dance Parisian Girls, dance!
and they danced thusly, and on such a day.

Is there a force that can destroy the world?
The Day The Earth Stood Still wants to know.

I want to know. The guy in the hat, he wants
to know. The old lady with the cabbage,
she's OK. Doesn't really want to know. But

The cars on the street are all black.

Oh is what they say.

Oh to be born in time.

Uh Oh.

I want to be across the street to think.

Tomorrow, I wonder, when the earth stands still,

Where will I buy my fresh fruit, frankfurters,
and drinks?

Where will I find a creature filled with a destiny
to hold my hand?

DIVERSIONS

Writers want to say simple things like "I love you"
but they don't know how. They used to. But now
they start to say "I love you" but before they do
a fire truck races by.

RONDO À LA PUNCH LINE

The punch line is the dessert of the poem.
I always tell it first in case I forget it later.
They say old people do this with dessert.
Broccoli, they say, is dessert.

Let me say this again.

Broccoli, they say, is dessert.
They say old people do this with dessert.
I always tell it first in case I forget it later.
The punch line is the dessert of the poem.

B+

You have been around all this time and you have never heard of a
_____?

I have been around for a long time and I never have.
It looks like a phone booth.
I think you should call it a phone booth.
That would be simpler.

We argued about whether or not it looked like a phone booth.
She said I was an idiot and I said I was not an idiot.

"I am not an idiot!" I screamed, and turned over the refreshment tray.
"My cucumbers!" she screamed.

I remember this entire conversation except for one word.

LIFTING THE SUN

Put me in the ring on your little finger.
Point this way (to the ocean) and I will say "Let's go!"
Point that way (to your heart) and I will say "How is it?"

I want to be this sailor on the open sea
Laugh at the wind for what's there to fear

oh you surgeon who can do anything
oh you love and save lives and caress
the living with hands called useful

LOVE IS

Tungsten is strong, looks strong, feels strong,
by God, is strong, I feel

weak, *debile,* fragile and like a potato chip
in love I shouldn't stand in the shadow of steel
the brilliance of its authority is paralyzing
like the sun when it laughs at your wife

I LOVE A GIRL WHO SNORTS

And burps and howls and kisses
like an angel might
kiss you as you lay dying

Also, once, a funny sound commenced
from her bottom. *"Allez!"* It announced *après;*
"Oops!" she parried, divine. All was well and I was

Dead for sure, but frankly, honestly,
happy I was, and even more than slightly–
I felt divine.

KIERKEGAARD TAKES A BREAK

I used to comfort myself
that Kierkegaard did nothing
but write and walk around the block
in the afternoon

But I don't even know the word
for 'block' in Danish and whether
or not Denmark even has them

And I realized in every way
I am a failure although recently
I met a nice girl

And she invited me over for dinner
and we had Rosemary Triscuits
and we had Michelob Ultra

And we had Turkey sandwiches,
cold cucumbers, tenderly assembled

and no one needed
to know
if this was really it
or not
and if it was

whether or not
we ever
walked
around the block
(we did)

SECRETS

If it weren't for her
I never would have known

that donkey noses look
like happy ghosts, frosted

that a daddy's feet are humongous
that a broken wasp wing can be fixed

that a big star rests in–
of all places–the back of a car.

Mostly, though, if it weren't for her
I never would have met her.

GLOVES

I was surprised how the donkeys
ate from her hand.

It's amazing that they never
bite you, I said.

But, she said they do,
all the time,

I wondered why she didn't
wear gloves

Until I saw her laughing
until I saw the donkeys laughing

And biting was quite the rage
in those days of donkeys

And no gloves and so much glory
and joy and chomping and apples

and biting and of course
love of biting

IT WAS A PLACE WITH TWO TELEVISION SETS

It is odd to have two television sets

One television set, yes, one hundred television sets, yes

Two television sets, I just don't know

about this soccer match in Italy

on one television set it says "Mario meets Guapi"

I cannot fathom why

on the other television set, a man with big eyebrows

the size of Mars

sports a black fiberglass arm brace dontcha know

that fiberglass is neither a nut nor a grape?

I didn't know that

the brace wasn't used for bowling, or golf, or anything handy

like sweeping the Taj Mahal Hell

someday I would enjoy a visit to the Taj Mahal

and here is why: one thousand elephants.

One thousand elephants with one thousand tails

Two thousand eyes have one thousand elephants

And each and every one of them helped to build this magnificent edifice

Their eyes were filled with tears

running down Eddie's face

Roughly one thousand. Jewelry stolen from Britain, but anyway...

It's used for living this brace. It's called an i-limb. Adorning the arm

of Mister Mars Brows. I-limb. Oh-i-limb–

'I' stands for isotope (radioactive) Iris (circular structure or rainbow)

or just plain ME. I end where I begin, where two is too many

and also not enough. I take this guff. This love of things

pray it will be alive and ruff. Turn on the television set.

I want to see your eye disappear into a tiny dot middle.

One is not enough. Two is too many. A hundred...

If not. Why Hell.

Why not.

MELVIN

There is a black hole
in a galaxy that begins
with the letter 'P'

The music of the black hole
is 57 octaves below
middle C

There was a man who sang
very low in a band simply
known as The Temptations

He sang: *Ball of Confusion*
That's What The World Is
Today

And when he died he flew
swiftly towards the galaxy
of low notes

It begins with the letter P
and is so far away he is still
not there. He whistles

To pass the time.
But there's no time
out there and no air
out there

And all the suns
are hot hot red hot
and canary yellow

All of this that isn't
there is what

all the whistling is
all about

THE SABBATH

for Faye

Is tomorrow Tuesday already?
I like the sound of that.
So I will say it again.

Today is Monday. Who is knocking
so anxiously on the door?
It must be Tuesday.

I don't like the sound of that.
I do not will not.

Over the crest of the hill, yonder–
I see the blonde hair of Wednesday–

I sigh.

AT THE CROSSROADS

(I dream of resting upon her pork shoulder
in a field of baby greens.)

(I dream of dressing a duck like a ham.)

My eyes feel creamy and red and crispy.
(My thoughts are jumbo, lumpy and somewhat yellow.)
(And peppery.)

One must be warm and orange, but I am
pickled, cured and home-made (my mother said.)

Something else my mother said: *Mostarda.*
You are my son and I love you, *Mostarda.*

(But isn't Mostarda a girl's name, Niçoise?)

I love you too, mother.
(I eat your eggs.)

PASSING FANCY

Before you wrote a thing,
you read someone else
and you loved someone else.

You read what they wrote,
and you loved them.
And you loved them so

that you wrote. And you
wrote and wrote and wrote.
And eventually, you loved

what you wrote and you loved
yourself, too, you loved
yourself and what you wrote
more than anyone
else. But that's not the point:

the point is, you loved someone
else first. You were many things,
wonderful things,

But you weren't your first love.

GOODBYE HEART

Every time I hear the cowbell that begins
Hello Mary Lou, I say to myself: Please
don't die too young, Ricky Nelson

But he smiles
and he does
every time.

THE LAST FIRST DATE

If the highway is a ribbon
what is it tied around?

More importantly,
what is the sky if not

old movies that you can
take pictures of?

But why take a picture
of an old movie
speeding out of control

tied around a gift
that is to big to carry

to June's house with
a fresh bottle of wine?

THUNDERBIRD

I loved her so much
that when I heard someone
found her textbooks in the trunk
of a Thunderbird well
I wanted them until it hurt

They were her textbooks
she might have drawn pictures of stars
or a dead boy's funny joke
her name printed with a daisy

Even if she didn't
they were her textbooks
I wanted them even if
they could have nothing
You could *flambé* that

Thunderbird if you wanted
it would take forever to *flambé*

They were so big and beautiful
everyone loves a Thunderbird
I venture she did, too, so much
she forgot things

But the last thing I need is
a Thunderbird
The first thing I need is–

Open the trunk and find out
What is the purpose of a sunken treasure
Its bed not of barnacles or bones of clay
if not to...

that's a textbook explanation for affection
that reveals the ache you feel you do
for something that hops away so far

a textbook

a feather

like a joke, hidden
punchline free I say

I just want the joke
I just want the joke

REQUIEM FOR A TERRIBLE ACCIDENT

Everyone enjoyed his smile and cheery
greetings in the morning. His Chinese wife and
his nice dog. The way he say Yay! to fireflies.
His brown hair. His shiny bike and his so very
dainty looking helmet.

PLEASURE SEEKERS

Never ask for a show of hands
in an empty room
filled with sponges and fingers

Ask instead for a gesture
Dress nicely and know

That a *come hither* will come
your way

and that rain will cover the earth

THE ICE CREAM REMEDY

I have a remedy for the insane: ice cream. Lots and lots of ice cream.
It's hard to be insane when you are eating ice cream. Well, let's say this:
you don't know someone is insane when they are eating ice cream
because there is nothing more sane than eating ice cream. And besides,

it's hard to say things, insane things, when your mouth is filled with sugar
and milk and cream and butter and eggs and salt. And what about peach
and lime and pecan and caramel and black raspberry and peppermint
stick? Yes, they're fine, too. Very fine. What is the most

sane ice cream, you ask? Chocolate, naturally. The most insane, you ask?
Balsamic Strawberry Bacon. What is the most sane thing you can say when
you are eating ice cream? "How about some more ice cream?"
What is the most insane thing you can say when eating ice cream?
"How about no more ice cream?" What if you don't want to be either?

Watch us, eating ice cream. We are medium. We say: "We neither want,
nor do not want, more ice cream." We enjoy lying and ice cream. Mmm.
We are liars.

APPROACHING GOODNESS

The world is warm and the clouds touch the horizon in a straight line.
I imagine someone very large, not like God-large, but large, like a bear,
running a rubber spatula along the surface of the bottom of the clouds.
It's coconut chiffon! he screams, and then gobbles it up completely.
He has a sweet tooth, and it has led to this: no more clouds today.
And without the clouds it feels like night. And when it feels like night,
everyone falls asleep. It's a good thing that things that a bear like to
sleep. It's a good thing there are bears.

I LIKE TOOTHBRUSHES

I like toothbrushes
now that they resemble

Angry Vagina Monsters
from a Ray Harryhausen film

How clever Ray was! if only
he could have seen these

toothbrushes before he died.
I would have given up my own

life if Ray Harryhausen could
have seen these toothbrushes
Honest I would, or a toothbrush

If I did

Ray could have made the most
wonderful movie: *The Golden
Voyage Of Toothbrush*

for example, or *20 Million
Miles To My Molars*. He could
have borrowed my toothbrush
I wouldn't need anymore,

The bristles so lean and soft.
The colors of this movie so
as you would imagine, given

the era of great movies. The
models: my toothbrushes.

Ray movies:

great, pearly white, gleaming

me:

bones

AFTERNOON PAINTING

I woke up thinking of my painting of Jesus.
His eyes were so blue and his hair so golden.
In the afternoon, the light would stream through
the blinds and make his hair more golden
and his eyes more blue. In the afternoon,

you could hear the children playing in the trees
but the mailman's cart was long gone by then,
and so was the milkman's. There was a lonely
feeling in the air, knowing that no one would be

knocking on the door, that no one would be bringing
you anything, even though the light streamed in through
the blinds, and Jesus' hair was even more golden than it
was in the morning, and his eyes even more blue.

OSCAR

I wanted to write something beautiful, because it was late
and I was alone and Oscar Wilde.

I thought of the madness of kissing, places that were hot
and colored, red and yellow wine letters, the wings

that shadow me. And then I found London–"a desert
without your dainty feet" and I thought:

perfect, delicious, obscure, and cosmopolitan! But
who wants that? I do, but only if it brings me you:

alone, absolute, illiterate with words

"Always, devotedly, yours..."

MILK BONES

When I walk towards your soul I feel
a dog barking in my heart. I hear FETCH
and I walk even faster. Distance to me
is an avenue of Milk Bones. My master
is far away and calling me thither.

This avenue, these Milk Bones,
this thither—I know this is happiness.
Or folly? Please tell me I am wrong
with a rolled up newspaper. How
gaily will I laugh with your wrongness!

Please join me.
I am so happy.
Can you? Please?
Or can't you?

NUTS

There was a little shop on Second Avenue that sold nothing but nuts.
It was called NUTS. Things were simple back then. My mother
would buy me nuts. I would point to them and ask "Why are they red?"
My mother would say "Because." That was also why the sun was yellow.
Why daisies were called daisies. Why the 'P' is often silent. And why
that man murdered all those girls and then went on THE DATING
GAME. When I asked her why peanuts had shells, she gave a very
complicated answer. It was scientific and strange. I knew I was
growing up. Soon I would be thinking about girls. I asked what
NUTS meant. She told me about serial killers. She told me about
dating. She told me about THE DATING GAME. I said, no, that
can't be. Yes it can. Why? Because. But Why? Nuts, she said. Nuts.
Just Nuts.

REAL

I saw the old lady wind up her hose. I heard the Mexican man laugh
when I asked for chicken. I forgot to buy a chocolate bar at the store.
I walked by the Glutino and laughed. I looked at the Izzy Cream Soda
and heard Dan laugh behind me when I said Glutino. I said At Least
There's A Breeze. I said I like cheeses as long as they don't taste like
cheese. I asked where the Feta was and the guy said right there
somewhere. I wept when the cashier said Have A Good One.
I walked all the way home until I found a German book. I couldn't
understand why a man named Kleist would write about beheaded
lovers separated by an earthquake in Chile. I read the mirror instead.
I turned on the television. I watched the Dating Game but just
to see a serial killer. I walked down the street. I saw that it was
sunny. I ate a Manburger. I watched the guy walk his dog with
what appeared to be an artificial leg. I watched a dog look at a guy
who appeared to have an artificial leg. I heard someone say something.
I shook my head. Dan said What. *I don't believe when a window closes,
a door opens. I believe that when a window closes, a smaller window opens.
And a smaller one after that. And a smaller one after that. Finally, it is
the size of a lemon seed in your sweet iced tea. A small one. A little seed.
You can swallow little seeds. A little seed will grow.* I like dogs that look up
at you. I like to turn off everything. Nothing is nothing. The guy with
the artificial leg? He was just pretending to have an artificial leg.
He had two artificial legs.

THE ROOT BEER STAND

The root beer stand was improperly named:
it also sold krinkle cut fries and hot dogs;

it also stayed open until midnight; many
young men drove their scooters in the
parking lot; the root beer stand was

not a root beer stand, it was

The Krinkle Cut Fries Hot Dog
& Young Men On Scooters In
The Parking Lot Until
Midnight Where
Root Beer Stands
Young and Free
& Longs To Be
Where Birds Tend
To Flee

Where I go to sing
this Root Beer Song

is a place where all
all Root beer things
and all Root Beer
belongs

Faye

JOSÉ BIENDICHO

Beat-up shoes enter the José Biendicho hospital
and shiny shoes emerge.

José Biendicho: or ⁻ 'Well-spoken Joe' ⁻ requests
the honor of the presence of your beaten up things.

If he cannot make a beaten up thing shiny,
he will weep, and his tears will make it glossy.

When you speak of José Biendicho, speak
of him well, as José Biendicho would speak
of you, as a once beaten up man.

HEAVEN

The problem is, if I go now
I will never catch up with you.
I just know it's going to be like
one of those super big malls
filled with sneaker stores filled
with teenagers. The guys are
always trying to impress the girls
and it's noisy. I don't want that.
But I want to go. I want
to find you. I will. I promise.
I just can't. But I will.

SNEAKY

What dress were you wearing when I saw you last?
Isn't it nice to know it doesn't matter?
But it does matter. If you are thinking
about the dress, you aren't thinking
about how long it has been since
I saw you last *but wait!*

I am turning around the corner.
You have an untied shoe.
You never saw me last.
I saw *you.*

GOOD TIMES

My purple fingers say
This isn't so bad
This life is pretty good
it leaves me where I am
it gives me fingers
and colors
and soap
to wash away
every color
but purple

OPEN DOORS

I was so foolish
I thought that all kisses came
from Paris. But then I discovered
one that came from North Carolina.
It had this pretty little blue tag on it.

North Carolina is a place right next to
the ocean and there is land on the other side.
If you look up, there is this sky there
and sometimes it's almost grey looking.
This kiss is like Bojangles because it tasted

like butter on a biscuit. It was warm in the way
biscuits love to be warm. Sunshine warm.
It was that kind of kiss not Paris not at all and it was
a wonderful part of every morning. Every morning

I would arise and wait for it to come to my bed
and ask if I was awake yet. Are you awake yet?
Yes, of course I am. Are you ready to start this
new day? No, please, I said, not yet.

FEET, WHAT DO I NEED YOU FOR?

Feet, what do I need you for when
I have wings to fly? asked Frida
Kahlo. Or is it Freida Kahlo? It

might be Frita Kahlo, like Fried
Kahlo, *Kahlo Frito.* I am going to
fly over to the library and find out.

Watch me laugh above
the clouds at all
the silly feet people
so far below.

Their shoes are red and heavy;
they touch the earth and let it go.

<3

This symbol means: I love it!
I thought it meant: once there was
an ice cream cone. It fell down
and could never get up. It melted
into a thousand soft pieces.
You mustn't blame yourself. You

loved it. They loved it.
Everyone loved it.
This ice cream cone,
I, too, once loved.

THE SEALING

The Mormons like to marry the dead
if the dead didn't have the chance when they could
I thought it was a ceiling, which seemed nice,
but really it is a sealing, which is OK too

When I was a little boy my sandwiches
were wrapped in wax paper
and they were not sealed
and I did not look at the ceiling
but I found them to be delicious forever

Marriage like a memory can be sealed
The Mormons say, Hey! marriage is a seal
It's not a ceiling and there is no glass to it
and it's good news because you don't cut
yourself and if you do! OK then

In this case I think there may be
benefits to that
more than, say wax paper,
which is only a memory
seals only vaguely and
is smooth as paper, which it is
with no edges and who can't love that?

It floats away and comes back
it is almost lighter than air

It dances where it wants needs to be and

It approaches the ceiling
with the utmost caution
but let there be no doubt

it does approach the ceiling

THE IRON MASK

When I told the Old Lady I was depressed
she gave me a copy of Douglas Fairbanks'

The Iron Mask

It is a silent film and the Three Musketeers
ride again and it may contain graphic violence
and it is digitally remastered.

There's good ol' Douglas Fairbanks
which means nothing to anyone
who doesn't know Douglas Fairbanks

So let me paint you a picture:

There's good ol' Douglas Fairbanks
with a tiny moustache and shoulder length
chestnut brown hair, smiling with head cocked
back and a forest green tight vest open to the nipple
area with one hand cocked on his velveteen pantaloons
and they other resting on his saber, slender and confident as
the swashbuckling D'artagnan, at the ready to rescue the real
King Louis XIV, imprisoned by his brother and destined to live
out the rest of his days in a dark dungeon wearing an impenetrable
iron mask to conceal his true identity: *ta dah!* the King of Damn France!

Now if were Douglas Fairbanks

I wouldn't bother with any of this I would
just get on a super fast amphibious motorcar

and go back home to Hollywood from France
and give dee-lish Mary Pickford a big wet kiss.

She was sweet as pie and more fun than iron masks
or motorcars or pie. Douglas Fairbanks,

what is your *schtick?* I can't mentalize your
brain-thoughts. I mean, really, what is going on

with you? Why do some people have problems?
I don't have these problems and I am glad.

Thank you, Old Lady, I feel less depressed now.

TARDY POSTCARD

When they demolish your house,
I want to be there.

When they treat you for death,
I want to hear that you feel great.

When that guy beans you with a baseball,
I want to be able to say: *Go Get 'Im, Tiger.*

When you forget who you are,
I want to follow you from the hospital
to the shelter.

I will be the one
with the balloon
that is red and fat
and no one knows
is really a satellite
for watching you.

I want to join you on another
earth that looks just like this one,
only smaller, and live with you
in a beautiful house—one with
the feel of a warm, kind toaster.

MUTT

From now on, the only movies I am going to see
must involve buying dogs at the pound.
But they must be mutts, not purebreds.

But that's ridiculous, because you can't
buy purebreds at a pound
and there are no movies that are just
about buying mutts at the pound.

I mean, buying a mutt for five minutes
ten minutes, tops maybe, but not the entire movie
but I didn't say the entire movie, did I?

But none of that matters anyway.
What I meant to say is that I don't want to
see any more movies. I want to buy a dog.

A mutt, not a purebred. But not a mutt
that wants to spend his days watching movies.
Or longing for purebreds, the kind you find

roaming free just outside of the pound.
This longing of mine, and it's an honest one,

could make life difficult for me and it's really
so difficult already. I might feel better if I had
something to love other than this difficult life in my life.

Like a dog. Or a nice movie. For instance,
there is the movie about a shark that they found

on the subway. It had a cigarette in its mouth
and a Red Bull in its fin. The authorities
don't know how it got there

and they don't care. They say that they have
better things to do with their time. It's not
a movie that one could really take home and love.
It's not really even a movie. But it is something
that might just matter to a dog. So much would matter–
a dog, a pure mutt, would care, and that is what I want. Care.

FINE EASTERN WARE

Do you suppose there really is
a Strawberry Street in Poland?

Perhaps my friend Dan thought
it would give me delight one summer day
as I washed my plates that he gave me

and turned them over to wash them
more thoroughly indeed only to read

Strawberry Street, Poland

and then to wonder if there really
is a Strawberry Street · Comma · Poland

on a warm summer day
as I wash the plates

and look out the window
and see what's there

and miss everything
in the world
that isn't
a strawberry

WHAT POWERS THE HUMAN HEART

Perhaps a diesel engine, with an oscilloscope. I couldn't tell you
what a diesel engine was if my life depended on it. Or an oscilloscope.
If they have anything to do with what you need for me to say, or do,
I am sunk. But you say, they don't. Don't worry, you're perfect.
Because you only have to be so good to be perfect, and you are,
and that is good enough.

WHAT DOES A MOSQUITO SOUND LIKE IN AUGUST?

Why, that's easy. It sounds like a motorcycle in your ear.
You see on the street there is a biker bar there, too.
You have never seen EASY RIDER, but you know about it.
And you know about those fancy chopper bikes. Cheap beer.
Dark girls. How fast bikers go on dusty streets and whatnot.
You know of the loneliness of the motorcycle rider.
You know of his despair. You can't imagine such sorrow.
You know they say that it is all worthwhile. They say that.
You know that is what they say with those teeth.
You do not know why. You can't imagine why.
And you can't imagine such joy. You can't imagine

buzzing in somebody's ear, or drinking blood
just for fun. You can't. Because—you just don't try.

DIVINE

This hour, when it is six o'clock, and the world doesn't promise
sunshine or clouds yet–but you

your gentle face, your soft neck–this is the hour that I love–
this hour is simply full of mushy for me.

BRING THE ORCHESTRA UP TO OUR ROOM

And we'll have eggs and vienna sausages.
Let them play *The Sidewalks of New York*
until we toast everyone we know until all that is left
of the world are the people we don't know yet,
all ready for our toasts, although they would never
know it, and once we do, we will know them,
in a way, but not so much as to be a bother but
instead a delight that we all shall someday, with
a hearty toast, forget.

WHAT I DON'T FORGET

The flowers grow out of a ceramic boot
in a movie that I otherwise ignore but simply
cannot at moments such as this. These are
the flower moments. These are the days that
defy the laws of God and explain the value
of heartbursts. It comforts me to consider
my remote control a portal to the flowers
captured by man for pleasant reasons.

A POEM FOR LOU REED
BASED UPON AN ARTICLE
ABOUT LOU REED
WITH ALL THE LOU REED
WORDS REMOVED

Coachella, Hyucks, Guffaws.
Chronicled, Cleveland.
Hoity Toity.
Trolley Car. Tiddly Wink.
Truly.
Daylight.
Persnickety.
Giggle.
Is.

MY CAR POINTS WEST

And I tell it we're not going west anymore there's no point.

There's nothing to see there but it doesn't pay any attention.

My car doesn't speak English and it just sits there pointing west.

My car has sad headlights filled with rain when it does.

At night, my car wonders where Saturn is.

My car sometimes thinks: *Mommy.*

Saturn is huge and far away.

And my car is waiting to go west.

It can wait forever if it wants.

We will not go west, I tell it.

I know. Me too, I say.

It coughs and coughs.

It stares at the night sky.

Try to be reasonable, I say.

It's not there anymore. No.

We're not going.

IF IT FEELS THIS GOOD...

I complimented the drummer on how he played Bill Withers' "Use Me."
He did quite well, nice and funky. Excellent use of the tom-tom. But how
do you go through life, I wonder, with a name like "Withers"? There's
only one man we can ask about that: William Harrison Withers, Jr. We
must use him.

GIFT

I received a Valentine in the mail
by that I mean that it was left
on my car seat by the wind.

But not by any wind. No.
This wind has a name.

This wind is Not, which is for
the best. And inside the Valentine,
which was not

wrapped, or a gift, was an oak leaf,
cut in two, by a night desert hand.

I gave it a kiss, because it's never good
to speak when you are inside closing your eyes,

thinking about horizons lost. This one good, this one
not. One kiss, two. You can feel where the wind was
not. This one's good—none are not. This gift

holds the name we look for,
for life we look for it.

BONUS POINTS

There are certain people who you understand fear mice.
When they are famous and powerful, it feels good.
It feels good like a waterfall feels good in summer.
It also feels good to say: "I am not afraid of mice, and
yet I am neither famous nor powerful." At the same time
it feels good to say, "I am both famous and powerful,
and I fear mice—but don't forget: though I fear mice,
I am famous and powerful."

And my hair is *wavy*.

LEFTOVERS

Next to a jar of peppermints
on an cherry dresser
there's your hair

Even when I turn on the fan
and I do love to do that there

I always say love to say
the same thing and I say
the same thing every time:

Brace Yourself, my Love!
For now we are on the ocean

It is wild and we will finally see
all the wonderful things

that we always imagined
we would that someday

we both will
and won't

JUST A THOUGHT

I wish you were right next door
And I was handsome and you
were the exactly the same
as you were and everything
was fine and we lived on

Cranberry Lake!

THERAPY

for Alina

Let me remind you—
triangles jealous of squares
can never be squares
without breaking bones
and rearranging. And
there will always be bones
left over save during times
of twelve but in times other
they will be lost for good
once there is a nice rainstorm
and the drains run free and easy
under the glistening clouds of terror.

BLUE MOON

It's too bad that you have to
meet someone to get married.
And that you can only do it
once a day.

ABC OF FRUITS

The A Fruits

The American Mayapple
is everything we want
in two or 3 words.

The African Cherry Orange
confounds us with its tipsy
and tingly juxtapositions.

The Amazon Grape both
beckons and repels; it is
a fruit that you buy and read.

The Araza purports to be succulent;
I detect razzle-dazzle: are they the
same thing—one outside, one inside
the mouth?

The Alligator Apple works too hard
to be loved. And then it snaps closed:
it's paucity of imagination city.

The Ambarella was never owned by
Victorian virgins; it protected neither
chamise nor soul, but like all that don't,
is delicious.

The B Fruits

Bilberry appears British; speaks French:
Billet-doux: sweet things done to Bill–
I appear in a Burberry eating a B labeled fruit;
I pause to take out a simple card; simply
by writing love, it is. I pause to crunch my mouth.

The Beach Plum: stares at you like an undrunk grape
but best resembles a plum earth, cold-hardy in drifting sand,
or are we? I think of a love now gone. I am restored by sand.

Broadleaf Bramble: it is what the hippies do. Do what you
do, hippies: scramble and climb! Find the top part of life's
fruit mollusk and pause to smile! Drink beer from the pitcher
called Broad! How edible is a leafy tasty jam? One *beaucoup.*

Black Sapote: a small genius fruit. Its floppy white hat
lulls you into a slumber. If you are waiting for bad news,
it's no longer here. I mean, it was, and then it went away.

The C Fruits

Cudrang: do not over water or mispronounce.
Revel in the rubberiness; indulge your face
in the silky texture. Wake up and find out,
Hey, I am in China. But at least I am filled
with Cudrangs upon Cudrangs.

Conkerberry: what my Mommy used to call me.
She thought she made it up. What a Cocoplum
she was. And I, her son, to whom she sang.
Conkerberry, oh conkerberry.

STAGE ONE

If you were here, I would nudge you
and say Wake Up, Look how funny
a runner looks before dawn, holding
a flashlight. The light goes up and down
and all over the place, and there he is
jiggling up and down, waiting for a car
to pass. He looks a little peeved. Now
he's downright peckish. Wake up,
I would say, you will love this, wake up.

WHAT WE TALK ABOUT WHEN WE TALK ABOUT LOVE

If we keep naming everything,
pretty soon there will be no more
thingamajigs. Where will that leave us?
she asks, pointing to her heart.

FRANK SINATRA JUST SAID

Frank Sinatra just said on the album
that it sounds like a different album.

I bet he didn't know that his private
musing would resonate in Snow Hill,

North Carolina, in August '13. Why don't
you have a look around and see what

you see, I might venture to say. Truly, it *is* a different
album here. Here we have a bird making a terrible

squawk and some kind of running faucet.
An exceptionally warm morning, a dog, *sans*
teeth, and a mailman named Barbara.

There you have Felix, who twirls knobs,
the word blonde and its mirror, a zesty collection—
a different album, lost cigarettes, sun on the piano.

AIR CONDITIONER

Late at night the lion roared (I named him "Air Conditioner")
and I listen to *Can I Take You Out Tonight* by Luther Vandross,
the 54th best singer in the world–and I think of you. But what
would you think of this? My thinking of you when you aren't here,
my mistaking an air conditioner for a lion, and the way I never cry
when Luther Vandross says *When I say goodbye it's never for long,*
because I believe in the power of love on stage in his Luther Vandross
wheelchair, with his Luther Vandross voice, smiling, bold, proud,
not saying goodbye at all, not with us for very much longer?

COOKIE POEMS

i

Look at me!
All dressed up like a Fig Newton.
Why with my beige overcoat from England
and my figgy-brown sweater vest from Nabisco.
It's snowing and I am going to walk down the stairs
to see my date. But if I am eaten alive by children
in this book, there will be no date tonight.

ii

My date's more beige than I am! She is asking for
my love. And then something about her socks.
Where did I put my hosiery? An excellent day!
Nobody ate me. Nobody even tried.
There's my date! I would like to kiss her
smack dab in the sugar wafer!

THE NATURAL

I had this nine second dream
in the middle of watching
THE NATURAL somebody
called me and said Faye is fine
she is just in the hospital
she's laughing and carrying on
asking for a hug and going on
about lambs that fly and such
so don't fuss and I said, Great,
let's go see her right now, you see,
there was nothing to worry
about after all, OK then, here
we go let's go and then

Robert Redford gave
a little wink, and took
a big swing and that
baseball smashed into
the stadium lights and
everyone cheered and

it was the best day ever
and everything was magical
and everyone was beautiful
Faye was laughing
and the entire world sparkled

with life it really seemed
that way in that Natural
dream it really seemed that way

DEAR SINE WAVE,

I remember when I first discovered you it was so exciting.
I felt just like I was on a roller coaster. Later, it was a
mountain range, but I didn't know your name. I would
go up, and then I would go down and then I would go up,
like a roller coaster. But I always ended up at the same place.
At first I was really happy and then I wondered: *who are you? why
are we here?* I thought you were my reason for happiness and then
I realized that you were really just a sine wave. An upside down
mountain. Going up and down like a roller coaster and staying the same.
A smile and then a frown. That's nice. You always seemed right side up
to me. We really didn't have to go anywhere new.

And then I moved to the desert. I thought about you.

Love,

Ricky

ANIMAL POWER

Last night my wife
broke the dishwasher
and a river of sudsy foam
crowned the kitchen floor

Yesterday my wife
imitated a flock of sparrows
in the pine trees
near the pool

This morning my wife
gave me a gift:
a half of an oak leaf
pressed onto my pillow

And yet when people say:
"But you're not even married!"
I say: "You don't understand how
powerful my wife really is."

WE PREFER

We prefer bad movies
to good movies.

After a bad movie,
we can talk for hours
about all the things
we could do to make it
a good movie.

If we run out of things to say,
we discuss all the ways
we could make our new movie
a bad movie.

Once, on the way home,
we got a flat tire.

Naturally, we loved it!

PROMISES, PROMISES

I made a promise to a girl that I would
drive her across the country and see
the wild west

I am unable to keep that promises
and I am not laughing but there is
a kernel of a joke as to why I cannot

Life, I have discovered, and for this
I apologize in advance, *is* the wild west
in all its untamed majesty

and you can never keep a promise
to drive across the country and see it
as long as you are alive at all

TOILETS

Toilets that work aren't magical.

Toilets that don't work are magical.

They are whimsical and alive
and you can hear the blood
coursing through their veins.

ROAD TRIP

I wanted to travel every highway
I know the odd ones go up and down
the even ones go side to side
but mostly I wanted to be
a conquistador of numbers

A perfect place to start would be "1"
but with which number do you say "I'm done!"
"I'm cooked!" "I've had it!" "Enough's Enough!"
"Caput!" "Finito!" Surely not one hundred–

I often hear the same thing from stamp collectors
or as they like to be called: Collectors of Stamps
Just because you have the 'Lucky Lindy' stamp
doesn't mean it is time to quit–there's always
the 2 cent Jefferson or the 1 cent Washington
you can admire his sideburns–yes–he had them
but they were rare. Why, even Life Magazine once

spoke of Washington, of rare stamps: it was 1954.
The clouds were white and sometimes blue.
Someone was in office. I think it was Eisenhower.
And his health problems.

But now even that magazine is rare. As is Eisenhower.
Think of it: you can't find even the pictures of rare
things anymore: Life, clouds. You can't do rare things. Still,

Let's. To be photographed I want those photographs
to one day almost disappear. Perfect and unusual–
that is exceedingly rare.

AS RARE AS A DAY NAMED FAYE

Wearing a polka dot hat. Living
underwater in a pool named
Zelda. Saying: you can do this.
You can do this now. But
to whom, why. Faye says:
to you. Inside your heart
the sky shouldn't but does
glow violet.

COLLECTIBLES

Recently I saw an ad for paper flowers
and it struck me as odd. Paper flowers
are something that I haven't thought
about for years, and I assume no one
else has either. But often that is how it
works: no one thinks of something,
and the years pass, and then suddenly,
someone says, "How would you like
something?" Someone says I would,
and then that same something that
has been gone for so many years appears,
is purchased, makes someone happy,
and then goes away again. The next thing
you know, no one thinks about it for years,
and then someone sees it by chance, and
thinks, How odd.

LOUDON WAINWRIGHT III

I love him! I love him! she screamed.
And then she discovered he had sold
his guitar for yoga lessons.

All her tubes of Crest fell to the ground
and all her Mays would from now on be distant.

She was the last parakeet in the pet store.
Her feathers were made of wood.

THE BARKING OF OREO

At six o'clock I dreamed that I was watching a film of your life.
We only got to the part with the little puffy dresses
and the birthday cake and that big dog named Oreo
and then the sun began to rise in my room
and the sun began to set at the party
and Oreo's bark faded away
and so I pushed the pause button and woke up.

I lay in bed and thought about getting dressed and going to work
but I couldn't. I had pushed the pause button.
It was great. There was nothing left to do but watch the whole movie
all the way through until you caught the flowers and smiled
for the camera and someone who I couldn't really see gave you a hug
and you laughed and danced all the way to the car
and the car drove away and you were about to star in another movie
and you were about to do something amazing, again, or maybe even just
buy a pizza pie I couldn't wait to see the next movie I was so excited
I didn't know what to do and so I pushed the pause button.

FUN FACTS ABOUT THE COMPOSERS

Well, composer. Stravinsky loved Scrabble. Someone said:
>   how many points is Stravinsky worth? and I thought
that this was perhaps a question that Stravinsky asked when
>   he was playing Scrabble, but it was not. It could be
the end of a beautiful movie about Stravinsky,

but I imagine that anyone who loved Stravinsky would prefer
>   to end the movie in a way that is more musical.
Some people say poetry is music, and some people might say
>   that Stravinsky asking about the worth of Stravinsky
is poetry, still others might say

"It really depends on the answer." I don't think so. I think
>   it depends on what the question is—not what the words are,
but what it is. What does this question remind you of? Since this is all
>   about Stravinsky, I think it would be better to ask the question,
and not answer it. And then think for a moment or two.

Finish the movie with poetry which is a question a nice question

One that reminds you of flowers, not Stravinsky
>   but still
>   that's exactly who
>   this question is

VÉRIFICATION ORTHOGRAPHIQUE

If you spell "I love you" in French in America, Spell-check always tells you that you've made a big mistake in English. In France, Spell-check tells you there's something wrong with "I love you" in French, in French. People in France and America often say that you mustn't say "I love you" until you are absolutely certain, because it can cause confusion and regret. Saying it too late, they say, can also cause a multitude of problems. Somewhere between France and America, there must be a place and a time where "I love you" is right and you can say it right away or even too late if you choose to. It must be very special place. Some people claim it was discovered by cartographers of love years ago and at first it had no name. Today it is called The Atlantic Ocean.

838 WAYS TO AMUSE A CHILD

A yellow book with red drawings.
838 Ways To Amuse A Child.

Page 15: *a collage may show a house,*
partly covered by family members
and their possessions, or family scenes such
as watching TV or playing ball together.

For a moment I wonder if my family
ever played ball together.

I imagine my brother and myself
with a little whiffle ball.

And then my Mother and Father.
And my cousins.
And my Grandfather and Grandmother.

And my other Grandfather and Grandmother.

And their parents. And their brothers and sisters.
And their grandparents. And their cousins.

Some of them might have wandered over from
next door. Soon the whole family is there. Way

In the back I see Charles II. And then Genghis Khan.
Almost out of sight I see Abraham and his son, Isaac
a handsome druggist I don't know.

Barely recognizable, at the very edge of the lawn,
right next to the Ozies' house, is Jesus Christ, and
slightly to his right and behind, Eve, and if I am not
mistaken, Adam. Why

The whiffle ball is already the best thing that has happened
to this family since we bought a hammock that we never put up
for the maple tree which died years ago

The dog is buried beneath where the tree was.
Next to the bone we never gave him.
This is the sort of yard that seems to work
no matter what does happen, or doesn't.

Somebody drops the ball, next to the maple tree.

Somebody picks it up and puts it in their pocket.

Near the family tree

Is someone I see

Someone I know

Someone I barely love.

BEHIND THE CANDELABRA

It felt strange to listen to Liberace on the radio when riding a bicycle through traffic. It was 1967 and he was playing a zesty *Mack the Knife* as a waltz, then as a bossa nova, and then as a pop song and yet his fingers were sweating less than my legs are now. Oh, if only I could have Liberace's fingers attached to my legs!

How unhappy I would be!

1931

Three young boys smoke cigarettes and pipes outside of a factory.

Please give the date and the names of all three boys.

The name of the building and the name of the factory.

What each boy was thinking and what each boys was smoking.

Tell of the signature of the smoke.

The key to the soot.

The number of the sky.

The sweep of the eye.

The postmark of the lung.

Please give the date when three young boys

walked down the street, kicked a small dog,

lifted their heads in the air to smell the lamb

grilled by dead neighbors.

Please give us the date that three old men

cursed their fate.

DRACULA

I saw him at 2:00 in the morning
fifty years ago. There must be so
much more to him than that. But for
now, I am happy that this is all there
is: Dracula on TV. A tray of sugar cookies
on the bed. My father's knock on the door.
A radioactive hum that will soon disappear.

CRY MOVIES

I love movies that have no love or sex in them.
Usually I find that movies that have sex in them
mean somebody will get pregnant and then there
will be one more name to remember. Usually I find
movies that have love in them also have death in
them, because if you love someone and they don't
die, what's the point of crying? There's no *drama*.
You can't have someone crying for no reason, not
in a movie. Although I do remember this one movie
in which everyone was crying all the time–cry, cry, cry.
They were all strangers and they were crying
all the time. They were all crying because they
were all strangers and loneliness makes you cry.
It was the most beautiful movie I ever saw.
When at last they died because of loneliness,
which of course they would have to,
I made a new decision about the movies
I would from now on see.

You can now cry in movies
that I will from now on see.
But if you cry, you must die,
and even if you are born
half way through, and even
if you are young and soon
lonely and then die, I will
still not remember
your name.

FIDO

I might be misreading my Plato, but as I understand it,
since we do not freak out when we see things then we
have seen everything before. This is good news and bad
news. I like the fact that the world isn't freaking out;
I like the fact that the world is an old shoe. I am sorry
that I cannot say "That's news to me!" ever again,
although I suppose I could. For example, I do enjoy
learning that the world is familiar to me and I didn't
know it. But I had to have known it. But it seems
that way, so that's good. Still, it was vaguely familiar
to me, as was Plato, who I think I already knew
before I was a baby. He had coal black eyes
and a twinkly smile. He tickled me with
his beard of snow. There is an element
of confusion and joy to this knowing, not
knowing. This is the good and the bad news
at once. Have you ever been on a merry go round?
Plato once asked. Don't answer. There is no answer
to that question.

YOURS TRULY

Which reminds me of the story Dan once told me
about Dan's Dad, Chip, and how he used to water
the lawn every morning wearing a red bathing suit
and how all the ladies would come out on to their porches
and ogle and sigh and sometimes they would whistle and
commence to rub his mighty brown moist back but that

was thirty years ago and now Chip wakes up in the morning
and he gets out of bed and yawns and looks outside and then

gets back into bed and smiles and falls asleep again
and dreams of buying a red bathing suit for somebody
very special, ("Yours truly!" chuckles Chip) and he whistles
to himself in his dream so loudly that his death wakes up
the neighbors and out they come onto their porches
and they ogle and sigh and sometimes they whistle.

BOY TOYS

On my weekly camping trip, I name birds in the sky.
There's a robin, a blue jay, a sparrow, a mockingbird.
And then it becomes confusing. I give up that nonsense
and I begin again: "There's Ralph, there's Jimmy,
there's Ernest, and of course, there's Franklin."

THE RELOCATION OF GOOD CARGO

I thought of buying you a typewriter for your birthday.
If you have never experienced the feeling of your fingers
on typewriter keys, well, then, you should. It feels
important and fruitful. The noise is also a fruitful one.
It is similar that way, although in a less noisy way,
to a steamboat whistle or a train. It doesn't speak
so much to what is happening right now as it speaks
to what will happen soon–by way of the steamboat,
the train, the typewriter. To the steamboat: *where*
will it go? What cargo does it hold? To the train:
when it arrives, will important people find their way
to depot? To you: *when you can no longer type, what*
will you have forever, perhaps, in your hands?

All of these sounds lead to something that is startling
in a way that rattles your ribs, but no one remembers
when someone else's ribs rattled and how much they did.
They simply say, *I remember a sound, but I don't remember*
what, when, or why. I do remember, however, that it was mighty,
and it was right here, they say, pointing right *here.* That sound is
the sound of something moving, from here to there, for what seems
to be similar to a good and powerful reason.

HANGING IN THE AIR

after Wangechi Mutu

If a ball is suspended in the air, you can see its shadow beneath it.
If the ball is cut from that suspension and falls to the ground,
the moment at which it touches the ground it has no shadow.
Or perhaps it has a shadow, and it is hidden. Since it bounces,
the shadow returns until the ball touches the ground again.
Eventually, the ball rests on the ground, and by then, the shadow
is dead. It is as if the ball has strangled the shadow to death, and
a murder has been committed. The identity of the culprit is different
of course if the author of its suspension is known. It is of course different
still if the ball is the property of the person who cut the suspension, and
of course, one must ask whose knife it was as well. Was anyone in the
room? Were there witnesses? Perhaps there was some sort of a confronta-
tion?

One must question the motive of the individual who cut the string.
Statistically speaking, a majority of those who would cut the suspension
on a ball in a room would have no clear motive, or at the very least,
would not be able to articulate their motive in a way that is meaningful.
Of course it is also possible that after years of wear, the rope finally just
gave out—as a natural consequence of age and vigorous use. This can also
be proven statistically. Often in cases like this, it remains a mystery, and
all things remain as they should be, at rest bouncing will cease.

FABRICS

In a perfect world, the sun would wear a suit
made of silk. It would be blue, a complementary
color. But you still shouldn't look at the sun.
Why would you want to? You have seen blue things
bursting into flames your whole life.

WHAT MATTERS ? MOIST

Cooking is satisfying if you put all the parts together
because the individual parts are not. The first part
means cutting a chicken lengthwise. The second part
means dredging it in flour. The third part
means pouring oil into a pan. The fourth part
means placing the chicken in the pan. Then there
are lemons and artichokes and white wine and capers.
And then there is the idea of a chicken that you saw
in a cartoon. The sky was blue and he lived in a house
with a bed that looked fluffy. He slept all day waiting
for you to see him as a real chicken, worthy of love.

HISTORY IN PICTURES

It used to be a law that you had to wear
a top hat in the subway if you were a man.

One man wrote down the law. He put it under
his top hat and forgot about it. Others say that top hat,

of all top hats, was the only one that never existed.
Some say women would frown at men without top hats

in the subway. Others said the unclean air gave women a cross
expression and made them cranky anyway. When the subway

commenced, though, men and women forgot their differences and
sorrows. Men would remove their boutonnieres and give them away

to the women who were so cross. They would doff their hats
with great courtesy to the women would graciously accept

all kindnesses. The subway would off, guided by a team
of horses. Now some say the horses never existed.

Others say those horses can still be found. Some say
the flowers appeared out of nowhere, but were quite
welcome. Yet all agree that there was once a sound

of some sort. Some pressed their ear gently to the ground, and
listened for the far away sound that a hat or a flower might make.

THE FLAMING TIGER \

I had to walk two blocks to park my car
in order to eat dinner at the Flaming Tiger.
But everything happens for a reason:
in this case, I parked next to an orange car.
Nothing makes me happier than an orange car.
Someday, I decided right then and there,
I will buy an orange car and it will be beautiful.
I will park it here and fill it with golden gasoline.
I will name it *Fidel,* after the girl who broke my heart
and filled up so many parking lots, as they say, with
so many cars

that I will remind myself that even though a car is
orange, and even though it is mine, and even though
it is love it doesn't mean I can eat it or zest it or
god forbid–juice it.

As Fidel once told me long ago, kissing one eye
and then the other, you must do what is right
for you–bracing me on Sunday at last
for a Monday breakfast with absence.

FOR THE HOLIDAYS

My donkey is made of M & M candies
from Mars Candy Corp. which is really just a big
donkey factory. It smells like fresh hay outside
and inside it is redolent with rich cacao
and the smell penetrates my head shell and
beneath is really where all the chocolate abides.
Bray like a donkey and I will understand
that we meet in the soul somewhere in Mars.
Chomp off my head with Magic Mars Teeth
and we will no longer be friends
nor something much nicer
for when again we meet
I will no longer adore you
with dreams and hay and
the donkeys will cry
for the day when
their shells become fur
which they say
in other worlds
is the right thing
for them
to do
anyway.

REAL FLORIDA

I have a natural love of Florida. And when I saw an album today
of folk music from Florida, it made me happy. I did not know
that Florida had folk music! On the cover was a picture of the
Everglades. Surely they are not suggesting that people played
small wooden guitars in the Everglades! I once saw an alligator
eat a guitar. I have a natural love of Florida, but I am afraid.

Perhaps I dreamed that love. I only know for certain that
this album is real and that I held it in my hands. And that
Florida once was an interesting shape on a map I bought
at a gas station in Florida. At the gas station, the radio
was silent. And that's where I am now in my certainties—
somewhere beautiful, where Florida is as real as the hands
that are holding it.

ESSAY
for Dorian

The best apple for an apple pie is a Granny Smith apple.

But now that there are thousands upon thousands of apples.

There are so many apples everywhere in the world.

This is a difficult statement to make with impunity.

There are apples from Argentina, Chile, New Zealand, Australia.

I often wonder what states and countries produce no apples.

I can only think of Alaska.

I like to think of Alaska.

Sometimes when I am shining my shoes I think to myself, "Alaska."

Sometimes I wonder what the inside of a truck

A truck filled with salmon smells like in Alaska.

Or off the coast of Britany, is something I like to say.

And I do like apples.

I know there are other countries that don't have apples.

What about Monte Carlo?

It's a nice place.

In Monte Carlo, they wake up and drink champagne.

I wonder if they get up in the morning and say: We have no apples.

They must be very sad.

And then they drink champagne.

I am often sad.

Men with mustaches are often sad.

Everywhere you look, there is a man with a moustache.

Especially if you read.

Books are healthy.

Apples look like candied apples.

Sailors on ships often sail on ships.

I see a crowd of people there.

Now we have large ships

Large ships travel across the ocean bearing all sorts of wonderful gifts.

Pirates love gifts as much as sailors do, and are more ferocious than sailors.

Although some sailors used to be pirates, and vice versa.

Pirates are known for eating starchy food.

Sailors make jokes about barnacles.

Given a fight to the death for an apple between a sailor and a pirate,

you would have to have more information before making a prudent wager.

The life of a pirate can be a dangerous life, but how would I know.

It is worth knowing that an apple can be a gift or a commodity.

To date, they are both. Is there a third option?

Yes. There are oranges.

I didn't believe that they grew in Spain until I actually went to Spain.

I went to Spain when I thought about oranges.

I asked a man who lived there, who looked a little like Laurence Olivier:

Do oranges grow in France?

And he looked at me in a puzzled fashion

And I corrected myself: SPAIN.

He smiled in Spanish.

He smiled in a way reminiscent of Laurence Olivier in...

What was that movie called?

the one with the terrible chambermaid

the car ride in the country

an attempted suicide on the beach

the baggy dowager

the sniffy George Saunders

the aristocratic couple with bad teeth

the Joan Fontaine trembling constantly

the broken vase

the white roses in an odd row up the front of a dress

the address book filled with marquis and lords

the forlorn castle

the many maids

and the rain and the mustache

and the tennis racket and

the all-consuming flames?

Rebecca.

EXPLAIN WHAT I AM DOING

Explain what I am doing.

I am cutting an apple into four sections.

I am carving a wedge in each of the sections.

I am filling each section with peanut butter.

And lining the lips with almond slices.

Between each slice, I am pressing strawberry jam.

I am saying I am done! *Basta!*

I am saying This Won't Kill Me.

I am answering Oh Yes It Will.

I am bringing you something to look at.

I really am bringing you someone to look at.

Bringing things to you reminds me of you.

You are saying How Thoughtful.

Oh Big Kiss.

And wondering why we are so happy.

And why we fly like flies not birds.

A STILL LIFE

for Linus

A watercolor above my piano sometimes has
a witch in a house in it, and sometimes it has
only the wind. Sometimes I love it, and sometimes
I love it more. And I love it best when the wind
comes along, sweeps up the witch, the house, and
leaves us with a blank canvas, and I am three years old
again, and not afraid of ghosts, although I don't
feel that way, although everyone says I look that way
in the beautiful house in the painting where I live.

WARTIME

Chocolate Ices cost a penny during the war
but because there was a chocolate shortage
Chocolate Ices were replaced by carrots
which cost a penny. Eventually there was
a shortage of carrots, too, and all the
munition factories were then filled with
peanuts and the front lines were filled
with thousands of young bodies filled
with chocolate and carrot bullets and
the streets were filled with the weeping
of mommy peanuts and shells filled the air—
the weeping costs a penny.

A DISPATCH FROM IRELAND

They are dispatching my bottom bracket
in Eglinton. In Eglinton, they dispatch
bottom brackets; that's what they do in
Eglinton. As for derailleurs, in Eglinton,
well, they dispatch those as well, from
Eglinton. HALO! Here is your derailleur!
they ejaculate heartily–
from Eglinton, dispatched!

LUDDY

Luddy says: if you put a white sheet of paper next to the snow
the paper will appear to be grey. I say: draw a picture of snow
on a piece of paper and then place it next to a piece of paper
with no snow on it and they will both appear to be white
and filled with snow. Late at night, when you walk outside,
your hands will be filled with grey. The grey will not melt
until you are met by the dazzle of heavenly black lights.

SPRUCE PINE

Fill my pillows with spruce pine
and my pockets with money
that smells like spruce pine
and let's go out to a show
dressed like spruce pine
with the bracing *eau de toilette*
of spruce pine that inspires
us to greater things in the
big city that looms ahead
in our future adventures
the big city

looks like a giant
spruce pine tree
that someone cut down
and put somewhere different
so they could plant a bunch
of buildings woven from cement
which is like spruce pine only
without that classic spruce pine
aroma no, it's limestone
and a little carbon dioxide
a hint of glass
and a whiff of my
Uncle Toby's aftershave
Now my Uncle Toby
is not a good man
and he is hard of hearing
but man, what an
aftershave!

PRETTY WOMAN

The pretty blue woman who looked just like my dead blue wife
was really dancing the night away to the surf sounds of Los Straitjackets
on Halloween of all nights she even started to twist just like my dead wife
so much in fact that she tumbled to the floor which was a real rock n roll
beer floor and what could I do? I picked her up and asked if she was OK
and she laughed and held my arm and said yes, she was OK, and she
smiled and started dancing again and faded away into the crowd and
I said aloud as loud as I could say–It was good to see you it was so good
I am so happy that you're OK.

THE FOLLOWING POEMS WERE ORIGINALLY PUBLISHED IN THE PERIODICALS
LISTED BELOW, AT TIMES IN A SLIGHTLY MODIFIED FORM. MY THANKS TO ALL
OF YOU FOR YOUR KIND WORDS AND APPRECIATION.

Love Letter Fainting Over Years *(Metazen)*

David Ferry's Aeneid ii *(Lake)*

I Love Old Lady Hands *(Vayavya)*

The Truth About Ethyl *(Sheepshead Review)*

Ingredients *(Ken • Again)*

Wouldn't It Though? *(Ken • Again)*

Ice Cream *(Winter Tangerine)*

Tarzan *(Shot Gun Journal)*

Places I Would Like To Live *(Petrichor Machine)*

Conversation with Red Ink *(Construction)*

Cowboy Tommy *(Bad Robot Review)*

Bully Music Power *(Bad Robot Review)*

A Quick Note To A Friend *(Extracts)*

The Beginning of the End *(Kin)*

Four Mannequins I Saw Today *(Aperçus Quarterly)*

Oklahoma 1957 *(Sixth Finch)*

Tundra *(Construction)*

~!@#$%^&*()_+ Opera *(Petrichor Machine)*

Haute Couture *(Petrichor Machine)*

Who Are You Going To Take To The Prom? *(Arperçus Quarterly)*

At The Ball *(Jet Fuel Review)*

Bluebirds *(Spry Magazine)*

Dr. J's Dictionary *(PressBoardPress)*

Roger *(PressBoardPress)*

Make Out *(First Literary Review)*

Lady Grey On Ice *(First Literary Review)*

Yeah Yeah Yeah *(Thirteen Myna Birds)*

Let Me Tell You *(Harpur Palate)*

Lifting The Sun *(Scissors & Spackles)*

Love Is *(Sunlit)*

At The Crossroads *(Bare Hands Poetry)*

Passing Fancy *(Walking Is Still Honest)*

The Last First Date *(Pirene's Fountain)*

Pleasure Seekers *(Former People)*

Oscar *(Black Heart Magazine)*

Real *(Former People)*

Mutt *(Turbulence)*

Therapy *(So & So)*

Tardy Postcard *(Phantom Postcard)*

What Does A Mosquito Sound Like in August? *(Open Mouse)*

When she was four, Faye Hunter brought
a wasp with a broken wing into the house
so she could care for it. She stayed much the
same person for fifty five more years.